Library of

Secrets

Library of Secrets

by

Reba Jean Smith

Word of His Mouth Publishers
Mooresboro, NC

All Scripture quotations are taken from the **King James Version** of the Bible.

ISBN: 978-1-941039-26-7
Printed in the United States of America
©2022 Reba Jean Smith

Word of His Mouth Publishers
Mooresboro, NC
www.wordofhismouth.com

Cover Image by 0fjd125gk87 from Pixabay.

Tribute Page

Overwhelming thankfulness for the Lord Jesus Christ Who gave me this story to write. We, who are His children are all valuable characters in His Story.

My appreciation to my editor and publisher at Word of His Mouth Publishers for their support and patience with a brand new author. Thank you for believing in this book and its message.

Special thanks to my sister by another mister, Mardie, who has cheered me each step of the way. Everyone needs a big sister, and I am so thankful for her. Yes, I will give you a signed copy!

To the Lady Constance, I am beyond blessed to have you in my life, your eagerness to share the message that Jesus saves our souls and our sanity is so valuable. I hope that this book helps to spread that message a bit more to a wider audience.

To the Lady Matilda, you are so precious to me, thank you for the long talks and wisdom that you impart to me from your road already traveled.

Sir Theo, thank you for supporting this hobby, although you will never read one of these books, maybe you'll listen to one long enough for it to put you to sleep. Your help with the computer aspect of it and helping me get it all saved and sent to the publishers means more to me than you might realize. It would have been much more difficult if you had not patiently and willingly helped me as you always do.

Chapter 1

Could she do it? What if...? So many thoughts and questions filled Reba Jean's mind. This was a new stage in her life, and she wanted to fulfill her lifelong dream. What dream, you ask? The dream of writing a book. However, this book was such a mixture of genres that it would take just the right publisher and maybe even a select audience to fulfil her dream.

Her previous attempts had all faltered and been left unfinished due to her personal habit of turning every good idea into some sordid romance best left on the trash heap of failure. Reba Jean knew she could not truly do this alone, yet she did not want many people to know in case it never was actually published. Although her husband was supportive, his opinions often felt critical, so she did not expect much encouragement for this new venture.

She had only shared her ideas and visions with two other people while the plot line was burning its way through her daily life and bursting to be expressed in written word. She would most likely need to use a pseudonym because she planned on being very truthful, even if it sounded too much like fantasy or fiction. Too many people had their own ideas of what she was like and who they thought her family was supposed to be.

She truly did not want to hurt anyone or disrespect her family members or even try to compete with people's perception of them. It had been useless in the past to try to dissuade anyone from what they had determined her family to be. Neither did she want people to read the book because she wrote it or NOT read the book because she wrote it.

As Reba Jean sat down to type her first chapter introducing herself and her book to the world, her body trembled with nerves. She was fearful, yes, that's what she felt, FEAR!

Wandering away to complete a nagging household chore, Reba Jean struggled with her thoughts. She was probably crazy for thinking someone like her could even write a book. Her mind was in a tizzy; her body was reminding her to chill. Thoughts of failures in the past, present-day concerns, and future circumstances all made her have second, third, and fourth thoughts about this journey into the world of the written word.

Reba Jean made up her mind; she would just need to consult Lady Jane about this as it would most definitely affect both of them. Lady Jane was the curator, or would the more descriptive term be the caretaker of a unique library? Reba Jean would need to have close consultation and reference materials and especially guidance through this library. Lady Jane was the only person who could help her write everything, as she was the keeper of the family secrets.

Lady Jane sensed that Reba Jean was thinking of her. They shared such a symbiotic relationship at times, yet at other times there seemed to be a real distance between them. As caretaker of the Library of Secrets, she spent all of her time in this fascinating realm of fantasy, fiction, friction, faith, and fear.

This wasn't necessarily a secret library, although it looked nondescript from the outside. Inside, however, this library was very much alive and humming with activity. It was rarely calm, something that Lady Jane wished was the case more often. When the library was in full work mode, she often felt that all the noise and busyness would drive her insane!

Lady Jane had become the caretaker of this Library of Secrets, the curator of its quirks along with its trivial trinkets and mysterious artifacts. When she was younger, she really felt like she was more of a spectator than an actual supervisor. In fact, it seemed that she was only put into real control just a few short years ago. Before then, she was often at the mercy of Reba Jean's whims and wiles.

Reba Jean opened the library door and slid into its amazing vastness. It really was bigger on the inside than it actually appeared from the outside structure. Lady Jane had told her a few times that even though the first floor was usually all that people saw, it had a multitude of levels and depths. Lady Jane did not like to go to most of the secret places in this library. Reba Jean knew she would need to find a way to help Lady Jane navigate through the maze of corridors, construction zones, and concrete-like vaults in order to bring to fruition this scheme to tell the truth without anyone realizing it was an autobiography.

Lady Jane felt the ever-so-slight change in the airflow on the first floor of the library. She had a visitor; her first instinct was to hide between the neat rows of books that she had just finished straightening. There was so much comfort and a sense of completion when each book was in its proper place on its correct shelf. Too many times, the library looked as if a tornado had come through and left a wake of destruction in its path. The first floor usually was the safest place to be in the natural order of things. It was often the first place people saw, and rarely did anyone go beyond the first-floor area.

There was even a small lounge area just inside the front door where most people sat for a few minutes to observe the library or meet with Reba Jean for superficial chatter. Lady Jane knew that Reba Jean really detested the small talk that seemed to permeate her society and acquaintances. Lady Jane also knew that Reba Jean really longed for in-depth conversations, gleaning knowledge and perspective from wise counselors or well-experienced, mature participants in her daily life.

Lady Jane paused for a moment as a family album fell to the floor. Ahhh, the library was letting her know that her visitor was Reba Jean herself!

As Reba Jean made her way slowly through the atrium and back towards the shelves of books, she wondered what Lady Jane would think or feel about this very large interruption in her already chaotic world. Reba Jean knew that most of the chaos was her fault. She had finally realized just a few short years ago that the condition of the library and the health of Lady Jane were very much dependent on her and her lifestyle. She had made the decision that she needed to get things on a more even keel for the both of them. Their lives depended on it!

Turning a corner around the family albums, she saw Lady Jane sitting cross-legged on the floor with a family album in front of her. Dust motes danced over her head, odd humming noises could be heard, and dark ooze seemed to slither out of the book onto the floor and stain Lady Jane's skirt. Lady Jane looked up at Reba Jean with tears in her eyes, and her expression implored Reba Jean not to open this album.

Reba Jean gingerly sat down next to Lady Jane, trying to avoid the black ooze that seemed to slither around them both. She wanted to see what secret was trying to break free from its necessary confinement. As they sat together, looking at the family photos, the walls seemed to recede, and they were transported back in time to the moment captured by a camera.

It was a birthday cake with four candles on it. The picture of Reba Jean with chocolate cake looked sweet and benign, but they both saw into the picture. So many tears, hurtful words, loneliness, abandonment, and anger were represented. At four years old, just barely, and already, she knew something was terribly wrong with her family.

Seemingly unnoticed, the black ooze began to get warmer and soon had the appearance of soft, black tar. The smell of something burning alerted the two women that they were in danger. Reba Jean shrank back from the smell of burning tar and other unknown odors. She turned to rescue Lady Jane, who seemed to be drowning quickly in the deepening, fiery pool. Reba Jean felt so helpless as she looked at Lady Jane's rapidly shrinking form encased in hot black ooze.

She looked up and silently begged for help.

Those seeming, barely noticeable dust motes that had been floating around the library seemed to gather en masse over the two drowning victims and turned into a beautiful golden glitter that fell all around them. Somehow, in a matter of seconds, the golden glitter overcame the black ooze and turned it into a beautiful gold puddle of refreshing water.

Reba Jean looked at Lady Jane, and they gazed in sheer disbelief.

"Lady Jane? What was that?" exclaimed Reba Jean.

"That was the memory of when you met Lord Rabboni!"

Reba Jean looked a bit baffled for a minute, then realized that Lady Jane knew her best Friend by a much different, more ancient, special name. Lord Rabboni, as Lady Jane had referred to Him, was the wonderful benefactor that had adopted her just after her fourth birthday. He had introduced her to King Abba and had appointed the Overseer to be her Guardian.

Chapter 2

Another day of writing had commenced, and Reba Jean was feeling nervous. She had read this morning that although her life might be a book, not every chapter needed to be read. Here she was trying to make her life an open book; was she doing the wrong thing?

Other affirmations had come along to make her think that she was still supposed to write the book, but maybe not be so blatant about all the secrets in the library.

Reba Jean was scared to go visit Lady Jane today. After yesterday's almost catastrophe, she didn't expect Lady Jane to really want to show her around the library today.

Should she just leave her alone for today? Reba Jean was an expert at procrastination, so it was easy for her to putter around doing housework and scrolling through social media. No, she had a goal set to write ten pages a day for the next month; she just had to put her big girl pants on and go see what Lady Jane was doing today.

Lady Jane had been enjoying a quiet morning in the library, beautiful orchestra music was playing in the living room downstairs, and it was lulling her into a peaceful, catatonic state.

She really enjoyed it when Reba Jean turned on this music every morning. It totally changed the whole atmosphere of the library. Without this music playing on a beautiful loop for hours, the library was often dark and had a sense of foreboding danger hanging around. Would Reba Jean come today to see her after yesterday's incident? She didn't think Reba Jean truly understood the library, but by the time this book of hers was written, she would either respect the place and her more, or she would end up just as messed up as Lady Jane often found herself to be.

The door chimed as Reba Jean opened it... when was that chime put there? It hadn't chimed yesterday. Was this a good idea to announce her presence?

"Oh well, too late now. I am here, and there is no point in trying to sneak around," she muttered to herself. Meandering through the shelves, she ran her finger down book titles, a row of yearbooks, dictionaries, encyclopedias, and National Geographics, and peeked into a huge room of romance novels too numerous to count.

Reba Jean heard the beautiful instrumental hymns very clearly in here and felt such a calm come over her. She closed her eyes and lost herself in the peaceful melodies. She slowly opened her eyes when she heard a faint sigh coming from somewhere nearby. In the middle of the bookshelves, there appeared a beautiful sitting room with Victorian furniture and a lot of lace and velvet. Reclining graciously on the daybed was Lady Jane, half asleep, half contemplative.

"Oh, Reba Jean! This is just the best part of my life," she sighed. "Would that all my days and nights were as peaceful and happy as this."

The two women stared at each other laconically. Then, Reba Jean heaved a sigh and asked the inevitable question. "Lady Jane, can you show me around the library?" Lady Jane gathered her skirts and gave them a good shake as she stood up from the day bed she had been resting upon all morning.

"You need to realize something, my dear," she warned. "This library is not like those you've visited and checked out materials and returned. Every item in here is brought here and eternally stays here. You have brought too much nonsense into this library, and sometimes it's extremely difficult to keep it organized and cataloged," Lady Jane remonstrated.

Reba Jean tilted her head at Lady Jane and wondered if she was being a bit overly dramatic about it. "Show me," she replied.

The music suddenly stopped, the temperature dropped, and they both shivered. Reba Jean took a moment to gather her courage as she motioned Lady Jane to proceed with the tour. It was now or never, wasn't it?

This library was indeed different once you looked past the long rows of bookshelves that seemed to have no end or the seating areas that could be seen in various random corners.

Lady Jane pointed to the walls that you could dimly see peeking out in various spots. They seemed to be made of a very porous material, almost like coral. On the wall above the front door were two beautiful round windows that seemed to change color. She looked at Lady Jane but noticed that her attention was not on the windows. Reba Jean looked quizzically at her; Lady Jane said, "When the music isn't playing, the silence is deafening."

Indeed, the quiet was loud, but then she started noticing sounds from the outside, the passing of cars on the street, the hum of the electronics, the ticking of a clock. What was so dangerous about all this?

Lady Jane put a finger to her lips, held out her hand, and they started down the first row of bookshelves. Lady Jane's hand was trembling, or maybe it was both of their hands that were trembling. They passed a small patch of exposed wall, and Reba Jean felt it pulsating. She was fascinated, yet disturbed. Was the library—alive?

Reba Jean felt like she needed a moment to digest this concept. Lady Jane did not want her to spend too much time in contemplation. Pulling her along, they passed locked doors, and winding staircases, and hallways that ended abruptly.

"Slow Down!" Why was Lady Jane in such a hurry to go past all these intriguing doors and mysterious staircases?

Lady Jane wasn't sure she wanted Reba Jean to really understand how the library worked, at least not right at the beginning. Fearing they would experience another episode like yesterday's was an all too uncomfortable possibility, or worse. Reba Jean yanked her hand out of Lady Jane's tight grip and paused to look around where she was standing. She saw dust motes amplified from the light shining in the windows, and yet there seemed to be wisps of mist swirling around as well. How curious, where did the mist come from? She turned to look at Lady Jane, who shuddered and then exhaled in resignation.

Lady Jane quietly explained in hushed tones that Reba Jean could barely hear or discern. "The walls are very porous," she explained. "They let in everything, and I mean everything. The vapors are ideas, thoughts, reactions that are yet to be formed."

Reba Jean reached up and touched a misty tendril that was drifting her way; it curled around her hand and trembled in anticipation. Lady Jane held her breath; what would this tendril give birth to? Reba Jean released the tendril, and it floated back off into the air. Everything seemed to come to a standstill. Nothing had happened! What a relief!

They both continued to wander down along the bookshelves through aisles of tables overflowing with strange bric-a-brac. Their eyes took in wooden chests full of undiscovered treasures, beautiful tapestry hanging outside of mysterious alcoves, and then, there it was! Resting on an old, rugged wooden table was a very ancient manuscript rolled up and held together with a crimson ribbon. As they drew closer, the manuscript gently unrolled itself, ruffled its pages, and re-formed into a beautiful book embossed in gold. As the pages ruffled, they could see some of the print was in red ink. Both women let out a sigh; this was the most treasured item in the library. It had been translated over time so that now even they could read and understand its ancient wisdom. Reba Jean gently reached out and touched the Ancient tome with love and reverence. She knew this had been here, she had another copy down in the living room, but she was so glad to see this one was still intact and interactive.

Lady Jane was overwhelmingly grateful that the Ancient One was here and seemed to keep Reba Jean's attention. She missed the music coming in through the sound system, the misty tendrils were still hanging around, and she worried Mr. Insidious would slither in to interrupt their tour.

Mr. Insidious had been the previous caretaker of the library before the Overseer had put Lady Jane in charge. "Sid," as he tried to charmingly refer to himself, was still adept at taking charge and controlling what happened in the library at any given moment. He had let Reba Jean think she was in charge for many years, but he was the one behind the scenes, orchestrating the contents of the books and the stacks of writing material that was in heaps by the walls. He was very talented at making Reba Jean do exactly what he wanted her to do. Oh, he wasn't always successful, but he had more of a chance to slither around in here, especially when the Ancient One was hidden away and the music of Shalom was quiet.

Even now, Mr. Insidious watched the two women stroll around the library, HIS library. Oh, he knew Lord Rabboni was the new owner, but he had lived here so long; didn't squatters have rights too? Sid knew how to play the long game; he had been around long before Reba Jean or Lady Jane were even thought of in the timeline. He contemplated making his presence known; he could be so charming and persuasive. He really wanted Reba Jean to open those locked doors, rifle through those wooden chests, and unearth some of those things

11

that Lord Rabboni had made off limits. Sid slithered around the outskirts of the walls, watching, waiting, planning, and hoping that this whole book idea would be his first iron nail in their coffins!

Rubbing his hands together in unholy glee, he waited for the perfect time to make his presence known. Yes, he was here, and here he wanted to stay. If he did it just a certain way, then maybe the Overseer wouldn't notice who was really in control. Oh, to roam this library again freely and wreak ungodly havoc like he had done many times before; Sid was fairly giddy with delight!

Those stupid women, he thought, *they are just pawns in my experienced hands; I'll turn them against each other by the time this book is finished.*

Lady Jane felt a tremor go through her frame; she could almost feel like there was someone watching them. She turned to Reba Jean, who just seemed to stare into space. Looking over her head, she gauged whether or not the mists of muse would descend upon them. No, nothing seemed to be really happening. Once again, there were the sounds from the outside world drifting through, and silence felt heavy and deafening inside. This never seemed to happen before the book idea had been brought up. Usually, the library was so noisy and busy and chaotic that Lady Jane often screamed in frustration. Her job was never done, so what was this new sensation, this suspension in space and time?

Was this book idea a good thing for either of them? It would take them back through time and trouble, but maybe that was necessary and cathartic. Reba Jean stood still near the Ancient One, but her mind was no longer on its beloved pages or thinking of its Author. She was unaware of Lady Jane and had no concept that Mr. Insidious was even in the library. She just seemed lost in thought, which in the library was highly dangerous if it wasn't the right thought to be lost in. Oh, Reba

Jean would soon learn how very much alive this library really was and how very careful she needed to be when she interacted with it.

Lady Jane wondered if the tour was over for the day; she had so much to do in sorting, cleaning, and organizing. The last week's journals needed updating, and she really did not like to be under such close supervision. That feeling of being under the microscope was not a pleasant one. She squirmed at the thought of it and realized a misty tendril had wrapped itself around one of her curls. Uh oh, was this her doing or Reba Jean's?

What was the use, thought Reba Jean, she couldn't write a book or even get it published. She was a grammar paragon, but she knew some editor would shred her written material. The library was starting to feel dark and itchy and made her head hurt. She didn't get far on the tour today, even with Lady Jane rushing her past closed doors, locked chests, and weird cordoned-off hallways. Maybe she shouldn't be so demanding of Lady Jane or curious about this weird library anyway. It was probably pretty stupid, and she was just being overly dramatic about it. Reba Jean twirled around with almost a mad look on her face, made a weird expression, and started to say something, only to just purse her lips and twirl away. The sound of the library door closing with almost a defiant click had Lady Jane raising her eyebrow and reacting with the same irritation.

Then she caught the unpleasant smell of something rotten cooking. Her eyes became large as saucers as she hurried to find the source of the smell. Careful to not focus on any particular thing, she whisked along the next corridor and found herself in front of a large iron pot steaming away with unknown ingredients.

Why was life rarely boring around here? she thought to herself. Eyeing the steaming pot and not wanting to get any closer to the bitter odor emanating from it. She pondered what to do about it. If she didn't know any differently, she would have thought Mr. Insidious had been around and was concocting some sort of recipe for mayhem.

She wondered what Reba Jean knew about Sid.

Sid had been around a lot, especially in the early days. He always had friends and employees coming and going through the library. It often caused friction when some of his underlings would toss books onto the floor or leave black oozy footprints on the clean carpet. Whenever Lady Jane would get too insistent about being the one in authority, Sid's eyes would slant and glow fiery red as he lost control of his charming facade. He was beautiful in a very scary manner when he would stick his face in hers and remind her that she was the interloper. He could squash her like a little dust mote between his fingers. Yes, Sid was very powerful, she wrapped both arms around her middle and hugged herself, but Lord Rabboni was her Advocate. She would send word to Lord Rabboni and the Overseer to find out what she needed to do with this smoking cauldron of putrification.

Lady Jane came close to the old, rugged stand holding the Ancient One. She closed her eyes and thought of Lord Rabboni and King Abba. "Oh, Agape, please hear my cry. I do not know what to do about this newest problem here in the library. You, my Lord, have entrusted its business to my care. I beg You to hear me from your throne and send me some guidance."

Lady Jane wasn't sure when the answer would come; she only hoped that the contents in the cauldron would stay put and not bubble over into the rest of the library causing damage. Its odors were getting more pungent by the minute. She felt desperate to make it go away. Too many times, she had felt this desperation. Other times, she was in such agony that she wished she could just die. Why did Reba Jean leave like she had? Was this the result of their visit today?

"Oh, please, Lord Rabboni, please come and help me," she silently pleaded.

Lady Jane stood in front of the Ancient One and fidgeted. Was there something she did to cause this?

Chapter 3

Not really aware of the turmoil that had arisen from her departure, Reba Jean checked text messages, puttered around with her book, checked her watch, and wondered when she should start supper.

She wasn't really that bad of a cook, but some days it just seemed like too much work to follow a recipe or use varied ingredients to concoct something that would make her husband praise her efforts. They had been married a long time, but it still seemed to take a lot of work some days to please him. Long ago, she had learned that he was a perfectionist, reminiscent of her mother. She resented that part of his character. She had come to despise the never-ending cycle of trying to make someone happy who was just never pleased with anything or anyone.

Their idea of perfection was not even the definition of perfect.

Reba Jean all too often felt like she had married someone more like her mother, the bane of her existence. For years she had struggled with bitterness, anger, and betrayal because her mother and family were not the ones you read about in many books. She felt like she had more similarities with the old fairy tales that ended in horror than in the happily ever after stories.

Oh, she longed for happily ever after, but her reality was far different. She longed to be treasured, cherished, pampered, praised, petted, and supported, but no, that was not usually the case, and certainly not all at the same time.

He was a good husband, even better now than he used to be, but she felt like he did not truly understand her, nor did he seem to want to. He had his own perception of her and tried to mold her into whom he thought she should be.

Her iPad dinged; it was a message from her husband. It seemed often that when she was thinking of him, he would reach out to her. He could probably sense it; he seemed to think he could. The phone's ringing scared her, and she stopped in the middle of her book to take a call from her husband. He was probably driving and couldn't keep texting. She could multi-task; she was used to doing something while half listening to people. Her gift might be listening, but too often she was lost in thought and only barely keeping track of the context of the conversation.

She forced herself to listen to her husband talk about his day. This was her job, and she needed to find joy in it. She was to encourage and support him, even if she did not always empathize with him. After discussing her book and the technical side of it with her husband, she felt a bit more encouraged that he was supporting this venture of hers. Maybe, it would work out. She prayed that God would work His will and way in this endeavor.

Reba Jean felt like her nerves had upset her stomach, or maybe she was coming down with a virus. This was not the day and age to have a virus of any sort. She had nearly finished her daily goal for writing, so she needed to power through the distractions of body and mind. What happened to Lady Jane after she had left so abruptly, she wondered? She wasn't ready to go back to the library yet, oddly enough. This whole book hinged around the library and its storehouse of information, so why was she now reluctant to venture back in and finish this now insurmountable task?

Was it possible that the devil or her flesh did not want her to write this book?

She wondered if old Slewfoot ever bothered Lady Jane or caused her any problems like he did with Reba Jean. Her phone call came to an end. She tried to be a loving, attentive wife, it really was her heart's desire, and she firmly believed it was her God-given calling.

She felt a burst of frustration and exhaled to let it out. This upset stomach was probably making her lose her assurance and motivation. She should probably take a break and just eat something. Ugh, food; it loved her more than she loved it. She probably had some sort of eating disorder or digestive issues. Thoughts of the past and its scars always caused her stomach to churn.

Oh no, the battery on the laptop was about to lose its charge, and the television timed out from inactivity. Guess this was time to end her day's venture into the past and present and future.

It was well into the next day when Reba Jean decided it really was time to ascend the staircase to the library again. She wondered as she climbed what today's adventure would bring. Hmmm, this staircase seems longer than usual. The door seems further away than it did yesterday. "Maybe I am just getting tired and old," Reba Jean mused. She had left so abruptly yesterday that she knew she probably should apologize to Lady Jane for her attitude.

With trepidation, she reached to open the door to the library. If there was a chime, it went unnoticed, for the whole library was filled with the most pungent, disgusting, gut-wrenching odor! Where was Lady Jane? What was going on in here? Holding her nose, Reba Jean followed the smell the best that she could and arrived in the same spot she had left yesterday.

A black cauldron was boiling away, filled with putrid black and green ooze, spilling over the edges and onto the floor. With a large spoon in hand, Lady Jane stood slowly stirring the pot. Lady Jane looked up from her labor, and her eyes glowed with an unholy light. Reba Jean's side accidentally brushed against the pot—or maybe it had reached out and touched her. She wasn't exactly sure, but she felt such a feeling of frustration fill her as the ooze soiled her clothing and seemed to burn into her flesh. Reba Jean began to berate Lady Jane for the nasty smell and the mess, then resorted to heaping recriminations upon her. The more she rebuked Lady Jane, the higher the pot boiled. She turned to see the contents leaping out of the pot and swirling all around them. Lady Jane turned to Reba Jean, and with a hand that was more like a claw, she clenched her arm in a tight grip and began to shake Reba Jean in anger. The two of them shouted and screamed at each other and physically fought each other, trying to inflict as much pain as possible.

Without realizing it, the pot and its tentacles had wrapped both of them together in a constricting grip, and they were ensnared in the vile ooze. Still struggling with each other and then against the serpent-like tentacles, the women were overcome with bitterness, anger, frustration, hurt, and a myriad of other emotions and memories that threatened to drown them both in the roiling sea of black ooze. Reba Jean seemed to come to her senses first; she panicked and twisted away from the pinch that Lady Jane was about to give her.

"Stop!" she screamed at Lady Jane, "Just stop it!"

With tears streaming down her face, she reached out to Lady Jane and hugged her close. "I am so sorry, Milady. Please forgive me."

They both cried together in sorrow and hurt over what they had said and done to each other in just a matter of minutes.

Although the tentacles were still snarled around them, they didn't seem as tight.

"What are we going to do?" Lady Jane queried in a trembling voice.

With a huge, exhaled breath, they tried to break free, but that didn't seem to work as the tentacles were still ensnaring them.

Reba Jean looked up and saw the far-off dust motes swirling above the whole debacle. She remembered yesterday when they had saved them from the black ooze. She cried aloud to the Ancient One for help. Holding each other tightly with tears running down their cheeks, their strength nearly spent from fighting each other and the oozing tentacles, they felt as if this was the end of everything. They would never break free!

Just when it seemed so hopeless, beautiful golden strands began to cut through the constricting tentacles. The ooze recoiled violently and shrank back into the pot. Sooner than it seemed possible, the two women were freed. Reba Jean looked in wonder at the golden strands and saw that they were made up of holy words from the Ancient One!

Completely spent from their struggles, they held onto each other and then just collapsed onto the floor. It was stained blackish green but was quickly drying. Lady Jane tossed the large spoon away from them as if it was a viper about to strike. Knowing that they needed to discuss the event, they were careful to be calm about it as much as possible. Reba Jean apologized to Lady Jane for her attitude of distracted indifference yesterday and for allowing the cauldron to spew hatred all over them. She was starting to realize that whatever she did or thought had real repercussions here in the library. It was time to get to the heart of the matter.

Lady Jane knew exactly when Reba Jean began to understand what the library was and how it functioned. There would be a lot to learn, but maybe they could do it amicably. She really hoped that Reba Jean would get rid of the cauldron and not leave it there to ruin the entire library with its powerful contents. With that thought tumbling out of her lips, Lady Jane reminded Reba Jean that she was only the caretaker, not the owner of the library. It was up to Reba Jean to dispose of that nasty pot of putrification. Reba Jean looked around for a place to put the cauldron; she definitely did not want it down in the rest of the house. She seemed at a loss to know what to do about it.

"Let me pray about it," she told Lady Jane.

"Right now! Please, don't wait and leave it here in the middle of this corridor!" begged Lady Jane.

Bowing her head, Reba Jean silently asked the Lord for wisdom in dealing with this very real situation. As she prayed, the dust motes turned into a golden mist that was both healing and refreshing. Reba Jean and Lady Jane both felt as if they had been washed clean and salve put on their wounds. "Oh, Lord Rabboni, thank You for hearing our cry," murmured Lady Jane.

Hearing a noise of pages turning, both women looked up to see the Ancient One flipping its pages. They hurried over to see what the Living Book wanted them to read. The page flipped over once more, and letters glowed golden and seemed to leap out of the page at them. Why, it was an ancient holy recipe to keep the cauldron from becoming a stew pot of anger and malice!

They read the ingredients aloud together, "True, lovely, pure, just, good report, virtue, honest, praise…think on these things."

What a relief! They could tame the unholy beast that had threatened their existence!

Reba Jean mused over this for a few minutes; as she thought of lovely things, the misty tendrils gathered themselves poised for action. Lady Jane felt some trepidation. Sure enough, the more Reba Jean mused, the more the tendrils wrapped themselves around her. She didn't seem to notice until a book slid across the floor and opened up to a blank page. They both watched in wonder as the mist began to color the page. A beautiful scene of buttercups and daisies began to appear as the mist painted the loveliest picture. With eyes wide in disbelief, Reba Jean looked at Lady Jane.

"Yes, every thought you have is alive in here. The more you think on something the easier it becomes inscribed in a book," explained Lady Jane.

Reba Jean reached up to touch another misty tendril and held it in her hand. Every atom in the room seemed charged with expectation. Would it be a good thought, or would it be a havoc-wreaking calamity?

"Oh, Lady Jane, I don't think I realized. I am so sorry for all the horrible things I have put both of us through over the years," Reba Jean cried.

Reba Jean and Lady Jane sat for a few more minutes, gathering their strength.

This was a lot to digest all at once. They glanced at the cauldron, only to find that it was a beautiful fountain bubbling away in a silver basin of crystal-clear water.

Oh! Such a thing of beauty where there had been so much hate and pain just a few moments before.

Reba Jean's eyes filled with tears yet again at the grace and mercy of the Lord and His forgiveness. She stood up and touched the pages of the Ancient One in awe and reverence. It rustled under her hand; she saw some more words highlighted in gold....

"....be ye transformed by the renewing of your mind, that ye may prove what is that good, and acceptable, and perfect, will of God."

This library needs a real transformation, she thought, and it wasn't Lady Jane's job; it was hers!

"Lady Jane, please show me what needs changing in here," she nearly commanded.

They stood and walked through the books and stacks of reference materials. Lady Jane pointed out the family albums and yearbooks and suggested that they be locked away in one of the vaults. They only bring pain and anger and stir the pot of bitterness. Reba Jean wondered how she could write her book if she did not have access to those albums and childhood memories. She gathered them hesitantly, and they carried them to the first vault with a crimson-colored door.

Reba Jean stopped and set them down outside the door. "Let's just get everything we need first and put them all in the vault later when we are finished," she suggested.

Lady Jane wasn't so sure that was a good idea, but she wasn't really the boss, only the caretaker. Following a narrow path through all the stacked books and papers, they seemed to find themselves in a different part of the library. Reba Jean looked around and saw an open archway into a fascinating room filled with electronics, computer and tv screens, and all sorts of weird entities wandering around. The sound of buzzing could be heard in various parts of the room. She looked around incredulously. This didn't seem to fit in with her library; what was this room? Lady Jane looked at her as if she didn't know why Reba Jean seemed so baffled.

"This is the entrance into Sir Theo's library," she stated the obvious.

Sir Theo, his given name meant noble, bright, gift of God. She reached up and touched a book in his library. There were really very few books in here, but she knew that was because he chose to use the computer for everything. All of his data was backed up on hard drives and servers. She really felt out of place in this noisy, buzzing electronic beehive.

Sir Theo had chosen her, and she had willingly given herself to him. So much had been written in the books in her library through this marriage of the two most opposite individuals. She knew that she needed to be a better wife to him and to leave all the past hurt and pain locked up in the vault down the hallway.

She had read just that morning that instead of struggling with the expectations of what you think your life should be like, you need to find joy in living your life as it is. If her library was going to be transformed, she would need to stop living in the past and stop behaving like a hurt child. At this thought, she turned to look at Lady Jane only to see she appeared to be a little girl in ringlets with a petulant expression on her face.

"Lady Jane?" stuttered Reba Jean in bewilderment. Reaching up, she scooped a handful of dust motes out of the air and sprinkled them on Lady Jane. Lady Jane only sneezed and rubbed her nose on her sleeve. "Who are you?" asked Reba Jean. Lady Jane just twirled around in her puffy skirt and skipped down the hallway.

Who exactly was Lady Jane anyway? Was she Reba Jean's inner child? She said she was the caretaker of the library, that the Overseer had put her in charge a few years ago. Reba Jean knew the library was hers, and she began to wonder if she was losing her mind. She was seeing people and talking to voices in her head; did she have a split personality?

Forgetting what happens when you start thinking about things in the library, Reba Jean tripped over a book that had flown off the shelf and landed in front of her path. She stooped down to see writing appear in the book; it seemed to be an odd dialect. She squinted and looked and realized it was writing backward... she read the words that seemed to be a diagnosis from a psychology book. She was certifiable! Ancient books, cauldrons, dust motes, misty tendrils—she needed to get a grip.

Reba Jean ran for the door of the library, slamming it shut behind her. It must be time for lunch; she wasn't losing her mind—she was just hungry. She looked at the time and knew she had to vacuum the floor still, the mopping she might be able to put off for another day. She listened to the beautiful hymn playing, "Spirit of the Living God, fall fresh on me." It was soothing and calming after her crazy morning in the library.

Shaking off the nagging feeling that she had left something important unfinished, Reba Jean began to look through the refrigerator and pantry for something to eat. She heaved a sigh—the struggle to lose weight and yet be healthy was so very real, so everything had to be obsessed over, analyzed, and chronicled. She lost herself in the beautiful hymns, and the thought of Lady Jane and the stacks upon stacks of books faded away. "O Lord," she prayed, "please give me strength to get through the rest of this day in a way that pleases You. In Jesus' name, I ask, Amen."

Chapter 4

Reba Jean pondered over her book; she knew she was supposed to write this, whether it was published or not. Could it be that the Lord wanted her to write it for more personal reasons? Was this to bring to light something that she needed to surrender to Him once and for all? She did a lot of introspection on a regular basis, but maybe she was just pondering it and not actually acting upon it in a manner that was health to her marrow and bones as the Bible would describe it.

This library business was necessary, but the constant drama around every corner seemed just a bit too much. She was still getting used to the idea that what happened in the library was a direct result of what she was doing or thinking.

She did not like drama, although she had had some dramatic events and people in her life, both past and present. She tried to exude a calm exterior, especially around dramatic people. Most people probably thought of her as a Plain Jane. Reba Jean paused and thought about the irony of that statement. Was Lady Jane of the Library of Secrets really her inner Plain Jane?

Oh, what did it even matter, she thought to herself. I need to be more concerned with what God thinks of me and not what others think of me. Reba Jean knew this to be true, yet it seemed she always found herself comparing herself to others. She also had been taught from an early age that she would never measure up to people's level of expectations or their perspective of whom they thought she was or should be. It felt like a constant tug of war to be nice to people when in her head she was chastising them for their words, behavior, and actions towards her and her family. She shook off this sense of futility and spent a few moments checking her text messages and social media. She wasn't bored, was she? NO! She declared to the emphatic thought; she just did not want any more drama at the moment.

Besides, she had to get ready to go lecture other librarians on Monday, and she had no idea yet what she was going to discuss with them. She always waited for God to show her and give her the idea or Scriptures that she was to use to encourage them as they built or rebuilt their libraries. She had been so busy writing her book and dealing with her own library mishaps that she had not even noticed the week had flown by on a gentle breeze.

Last week they had discussed the use of pencils and keeping them sharp. Weeks before that, they had written letters and talked about getting to the heart of taking care of a library. She thought she learned more from these sessions than maybe even the other attendees. You really shouldn't teach or lecture something you have not learned or experienced yourself, she had often stated.

She felt a thought niggle at the back of her mind... she had left something unfinished; she was sure of it... Oh well, whatever it was, surely it would be okay until she was able to remember it or to fix it.

Reba Jean settled back with a ginger ale in her hand, listening to soft hymns playing in the living room. Ahh, this was the life she thought. She wasn't working away from home right now. She really hoped that maybe writing this book would bring in some money. She felt as if she had to prove to her husband that she could make money from home. Exhaling, she felt a sense of contentment as she looked out the window at the pretty view of their back field. She was a true country girl; wide open spaces, flowery breezes, and chattering songbirds all felt like a balm to her psyche.

It was just the beginning of spring, her new favorite season. Such peace and contentment filled her as she thanked God for letting her, even for this brief time, to be at home where she felt like she belonged. She wasn't sure how long it would last. Would she need to go back into the outside work world? She hoped not; she ached for the day when they could earn enough money that maybe they could breathe. She knew what it was like to not have enough to go around, but God had NEVER let them go hungry. She was so thankful to see how He loved them and answered their prayers over and over again.

She read over some of her last paragraphs, somewhat in awe that she was even writing a book. Oh, she had a vast imagination for sure, but never did it seem to just flow from her fingers. Would anyone she knew read this, she wondered. What would they think? Wait a minute; there she was craving affirmation again. If she was doing what the Lord was directing her to do, then other people's affirmation shouldn't supersede His.

Reba Jean really did not want to go back up to the library, even though she knew that she would have to solve the mystery if she was ever to have any peace.

The mystery, you ask? The mystery of who was Lady Jane, and why was she the caretaker of MY library? Reba Jean stopped and thought she probably was a bit batty after all. Here she was talking to herself as if she had an audience instead.

"Sheer nonsense, stuff and nonsense, no sense at all," seemed to sing song its way through her musings. Her laptop battery seemed to be lasting a lot longer today; she decided that she really needed to write more of the book and stop lollygagging. Words were such fun and interesting creatures. She loved to play with words, and sometimes she got to play word games with others. She knew that on a deeper level, she was just showing off her intelligence and education, but she tried not to think of herself as superior to others. She did not like feeling inadequate or stupid, so she needed to make sure she did not make others feel that same way. Reba Jean had to fight against an odd sort of pride. It was more of a defensive mechanism built from years of criticisms and reprimands for not measuring up to other people's ideals for her.

Her fingers flew across the keyboard, stopping to correct typos as she noticed them and wishing that she could somehow manage to type perfectly the first time. Part of her longed to tell her sister and some of her other friends and family that she was writing a book. In this day and time when people rarely read actual inked words anymore, she doubted it would end up in book form. It would probably stay in a digital format. She was old-fashioned enough to think about cover pages, cover art, and back cover synopsis... technology was good for a lot of things, but she missed the days of inhaling the smell of book bindings and seeing the little, tiny wood mites as she turned the pages of some mystery, romance, or adventure. Her husband often accused her of using run-on sentences. She was sure the copy editor would find some of those, as well.

She liked to type as if she was talking. Even though she had a penchant for correct grammar and spelling, she herself often fell victim to the same errors.

Was she just prolonging the inevitable? What had happened in the library after she left? If she was in control of that library as she had thought, then why was it in such dramatic disarray whenever she explored it? She needed to sit down and have a heart-to-heart chat with Lady Jane and bring it all out in the open. Oh, she would have to be careful in what she said and how she said it, of course. That library seemed to have a mind of its own! She sighed as she thought of having to climb the staircase again; it had felt so long and arduous this morning. Why wasn't she more excited to go explore such a fanciful realm? Was it because she had to literally see every thought come to life as it were?

Reba Jean mused over this morning's escapade, trying not to think of the black cauldron but rather the beautiful silver fountain cascading such pure crystal water. The Ancient One had felt so familiar and comforting, yet still like an austere disciplinarian at times. She squirmed and scratched her suddenly itchy skin at the thought of once again having to be obedient. Why was that so hard? She knew that Jesus loved her, yet all she seemed to focus on was the endless realm of rules. Her upbringing had been just such, "Do this, don't do that, behave, be quiet, get your work done, stay in your room, go to bed, don't go there, act like a lady…"

Act like a lady? Is that where Lady Jane came from?

Lady Jane sat in her boudoir, trying to block out the noise of books skittering down hallways and itchy tendrils slithering around her face. She tried to just concentrate on the hymns playing through the sound system. This morning had been scary, but she had been in worse situations, usually alone. She wasn't sure she wanted Reba Jean to understand what happened in the library; her presence or absence never seemed to improve the conditions either way. She knew that Reba Jean had left all those past tomes in the hallway next to the crimson door of the vault. She also had seen black claws send some of them skittering off to shady alcoves. Was she supposed to put them in the vault? She did not have the key. All vaults were to be locked tight, and even the wooden chests were locked. These were not meant to be accessed; they were filled with forbidden or forgiven events.

She heard a whispering hiss calling her name, "Lady Jannnne." Oh no, it was Sid coming to harass her. Sid slid into the room and flopped down almost on top of Lady Jane. His hot breath and sickening cologne made her draw back. He slid an arm around her shoulders and drew her near. Her skin crawled and itched as he twirled one of her ringlets through his long, tapered fingers.

"What are you doing, my Precious?" he asked with a glint in his eyes.

Lady Jane squirmed away, but he just held her closer. "You know, my dear, that battle axe is trying to get rid of you? She thinks she is so holy, but we will show her what a wretch she truly is. Imagine her uppityness in thinking SHE owns this library. We both know who the real owner is," he murmured with a hot breath in her ear.

Sid flung himself upright and looked around at Lady Jane's inner chamber. Oh, the things he could do in here once again if she would just loosen up. He really couldn't make her do anything she did not want to, but he also knew that she was not totally aware of that fact. He leered at her and stalked around her like a lion circling its prey. "Why did you let her up here, anyway, Milady?" he purred. "You know she will only make a mess of your organization; here, let me help you clean up."

Before Lady Jane could react, Sid skittered down the hall, flinging books back onto shelves, kicking others into corners, and clearing away most of the pile that had been sitting by the crimson door. It really did not look any neater; if anything, it looked worse. There seemed to be a fine gray dust or soot settling on things, and the air smelled dank and foul.

Sid was making her day even worse; she really wished he would leave her alone. She always felt violated and humiliated under his glittering eyes. Lady Jane whimpered and curled up in a ball, trying to block out everything but especially what Sid was doing. She heard him nailing something to a doorway—it was some sort of comparison chart. She wrinkled her face in confusion, but at least he wasn't touching her.

He touched some tapestry, and it turned a swamp green in color. Then cocking his head, he pulled an old vinyl record out of a crack and, with his long claw-like nail, started playing it as it twirled on his other finger. It was a sing-songy repetition of reprimands from the far past. Lady Jane covered her ears and closed her eyes. Sid just cackled and stalked off to see what else he could do to make the library more hospitable to his tastes.

Lady Jane rocked back and forth and whimpered to herself. Sid always made her feel so inept and incapable of taking care of the library or even herself. He made it seem as if he alone was the only one who could truly run the library. She peeked up to see heavy black rain clouds and a fog bank roll in; she couldn't even see the light shining in the windows, and she couldn't hear the hymns playing through the sound system as that spinning record drowned them out.

Sid was having a ball, redecorating and removing any sense of calm that had permeated the library after the cauldron had been transformed into a fountain. He really needed to find a way to cover that fountain and hide the Ancient One. That Ancient One always seemed to ruin a good time and quell his mayhem.

Sid had to be careful, though; if he did too much, they might be able to evict him from the sheer shock of it. No, he had to make it look as if they had done this to the library, not him. He blew a slimy kiss to Lady Jane and slid into the black cloud and out of sight.

Lady Jane shivered and felt goosebumps come up on her arms. That Sid, she was familiar with his ways, but she would prefer Reba Jean for company or one of her friends. Lady Jane thought of her friends, Lady Matilda and Lady Constance.

33

Lady Matilda was a real treasure of wisdom, grace, and experience. She often soothed Lady Jane or made her think and ponder different perspectives. Her outspokenness was a refreshing antidote for many situations she encountered here in the library.

Lady Constance was a woman of deep emotion and strength. Her excitement was often a boon to those around her, and her desire to learn the Ancient One's words was so edifying and challenging. She came to Lady Jane on a regular basis with questions and thoughts. When she saw Lady Constance coming, she would catch the excitement as they discussed some book together, but oh their discussions about the Ancient One were the most thrilling. Lady Constance was very outspoken about her love for the Ancient One and Lord Rabboni.

Just the thought of Lord Rabboni and the Overseer gave Lady Jane some comfort. Then she wondered what they would think of the mess in the library! What if King Abba came today for an inspection?! Lady Jane wished Reba Jean would come up and help her finish this project. This whole book deal was causing more chaos in the library than was good for either of them.

Lady Jane felt a sense of panic; maybe Sid was right; she was very inept at keeping this library organized and cleaned. Reba Jean was probably right in doing away with her. With a sob of defeat, Lady Jane flopped down on the floor and cried, and the black clouds overhead cried with her. She felt like she was drowning in her tears and the gray rain that was drenching her.

Where was Reba Jean? Where were Lord Rabboni and the Overseer? Did no one care about her anymore? Maybe she would just run away or let one of those scaly creatures lurking around whisk her off to the nether world. The room got darker and darker as she thought of killing herself or maybe even

34

killing Reba Jean. It would end either way for her; she sobbed and hiccupped. She did not know where the thoughts of death came from, but she was past caring. Where was Lady Constance or Lady Matilda? Why could nobody be around when she needed them? Lady Jane rocked back and forth and hugged herself until she thought she couldn't breathe.

Reba Jean was getting a headache, her chest hurt, and she wondered yet again if she had some disease or something wrong with her heart. She felt a sense of anxiety and wondered if her blood pressure was high again. She considered taking a nap just to turn the world off as she thought of it. She got tired so easily even after resting all week.

Her sister was trying to help her get ready for her library lecture on Monday, but she couldn't seem to focus on much. She probably ate too many potato chips or drank too much soda; she was so sensitive to food and sodium. It was discouraging not being able to just enjoy food and life without consequences.

Reba Jean decided to get a tall glass of water and check her blood pressure. Her chest really hurt, and she felt like she wasn't able to breathe correctly. Well, her blood pressure was slightly elevated, but not much, not enough to be concerned. Maybe she just needed to take her mind off the book for a while. Lady Jane was probably better off without her stomping through the library and making a mess of things.

After this morning and all of its drama, she would probably wait a couple of days before invading Lady Jane's inner sanctum again. Although she was curious about Lady Jane and felt like she needed to keep their relationship on a more even keel, she shrugged off the sense of anxiety and tension that she felt. Lady Jane could take care of herself, couldn't she?

Reba Jean looked at the clock and figured it was nearly time to just put the laptop away and get ready for her husband to come home from work. She planned on resting all weekend before she had to lecture the other librarians on Monday morning. Sunday would be spent at church, worshipping and learning, and she needed to focus on that more than she had been lately. She definitely did not need to be thinking of her storyline or plot or Lady Jane while she was at church. Surprised at how long the laptop battery had lasted today and thinking that maybe she should write a bit longer, she poised her fingers over the keys and stared out the window. Letting the current hymn playing on the sound system soak into her soul, she calmed her body and mind and thought about what to say.

"Fairest Lord Jesus" filtered into her mind like sunbeams dancing on a pond. There was still an ache in her chest but not as bad as it had been. She probably needed to get up and move around some more; sitting and typing all day wasn't healthy for someone in her overweight condition.

After some contemplation over the plot and still wishing someone else would read it and enjoy it, she decided that she would save the next chapter for another day. She thought of Lady Jane once more and hoped she was okay; she felt almost like she should pray for her. Was that weird? She wasn't even sure who Lady Jane was—if she was real or a figment of her imagination. The mystery of Lady Jane's identity seemed to be a secret in itself to Reba Jean. She often wondered if her library was in need of repair or reconstruction. Whomever Lady Jane was, she would need Reba Jean to be a godly influence and example to her.

"Lord, I know nothing is secret from You; if Lady Jane needs You, Lord, I asked that You touch her and comfort her.

Please, help us to have wisdom in taking care of the library; may it bring honor and glory to Your name, I humbly ask. In Jesus' name, Amen."

Lady Jane felt a sweet presence fill the room; the drenching showers were replaced with a beautiful rainbow that seemed to hold her close and remind her that she wasn't alone. The Overseer was there to help her do what Lord Rabboni had instructed her to do. She was to take care of the library. It might be a Library of Secrets right now, but nothing was hidden or secret from King Abba. He would clear all this up; this library belonged to the King! She was His humble servant. Oh, it felt so good again in here in the presence of the King's Overseer.

With a gulp and a brushing away of tears, she rose from her crumpled heap, shook her skirts free of wrinkles, and assessed her surroundings. Dust motes glittered gold all around her, the fountain sung merrily, and sunbeams danced through the windows overhead. Misty tendrils seemed to caress her body in velvety softness as she wandered through the library.

Sid had really made things worse while he was here, kicking things around and moving books that they had worked so hard to gather this morning. She tried to put some of them back in the pile they had made earlier, but she couldn't budge them. They seemed to weigh triple what they did before Sid touched them. What had he done to them? Would Reba Jean and her together be able to move them into the vault? When would Reba Jean come back to the library?

Lady Jane started to get apprehensive, but the strains of "How Great Thou Art" filtered through the room, and she breathed in the sense of peace that had filled the room when the Overseer had arrived. She wished she could bottle that peace or make it into a pillow to hug whenever she was feeling in need of its calming power. The day was nearly over, and night would begin again. Was Reba Jean aware that Lady Jane did not really

37

sleep? Lady Jane had a whole different task while Reba Jean slept, one that she knew would have to be discussed eventually. For now, just the moments of peace and solitude were all the rest she got, even if just in snatches.

What a day, but it really was no different from any other day in the library, except now Reba Jean was more active and involved with her. Was her time in the library coming to an end? Where would she go; what would she do? She had only known the library; most of the time, she had been a spectator or a victim until Lord Rabboni had appointed her as the caretaker. She wondered about Sid for a minute but did not want to think of him as that usually seemed an invitation for him to visit. She shrank from the thought of that. As Sir Theo often said, "It's the evils you know…"

Sir Theo, gift of God, how did he play into all this? His library was adjoined to this one. It was so vastly different, and yet, she knew Sid went in there and bothered him a lot too. Was it her fault that Sid bothered Sir Theo?

She knew better than to think that they should have a door between their libraries; Reba Jean had demolished the only one that had been there years ago. Lady Jane felt protective of Sir Theo and a bit sorry for him.

The next time Reba Jean came to the library, they needed to lay down a game plan for fixing its underlying issues. Glancing at the strange comparison chart that Sid had nailed up, she wondered what Reba Jean would say about it. What was Sid up to now?

She felt better, maybe it was the water or praying for Lady Jane, but the anxiety and chest pains dissipated. Reba Jean could even ignore the residual headache.

It was time to save her work and relax until her husband came home. She needed to be more attentive to him and less detached or superficial.

She did not like how she obsessed about things. She was obsessing about the book too much, but the plot was just burning inside of her trying to come out. She felt as if she wasn't able to type fast enough or long enough to get it all out onto paper.

What a day! She caught a snippet of the hymn playing "Spirit of the Living God, fall fresh on me," oh, how very applicable.

Reba Jean calmed down even more. If God wanted her to finish this book, He would help her do it. In the meantime, she had to learn balance and love the life He had blessed her with. Closing her eyes, she once again thanked the Lord for allowing her to be home right now and for the beautiful hymns of the faith that refreshed her mind and soul as they filled her whole being with His goodness and love. "Spirit of the Living God, fall fresh on me," she sang to Him.

Thy will be done, oh Lord, not mine; she ended her thought in another prayer to her Heavenly Father.

Chapter 5

It had been a crazy weekend of sorts, as she tried not to think of the book and the library or allow thoughts of resentment and frustration to dominate her days.

She had shared the first chapter with her sweet friend, Mardie, one of the only ones who knew she was writing a book. It was already Tuesday, and she was just now making herself sit back down at the keyboard. She had gathered some research and had proofread her last few chapters. Was it prideful to be enthralled with her own story? With banana bread baking in the oven and beautiful hymns once again permeating the house, she thought about yesterday's events.

Her lecture with the other librarians had gone pretty well. The topic had been "What Are You Doing?" It centered around what to do with your library when you aren't sure what your next steps should be. There was one young librarian in the group right now that just did not think anything really applied to her. She was slack on all responsibility and acted so innocent when her assignments and research were left uncompleted. Reba Jean actually understood some of this; she had felt like that years and years ago. She was also an empath, though, so she could take on the feelings of someone else until they felt like her own.

In the middle of her yard work yesterday, she received a phone call informing her that one of her dear sisters of the heart had just said "goodbye until Heaven" to her father. Reba Jean had dropped everything and drove over there with the hope to at least be a comfort of some sort. Later that night, she discussed it with her husband, and he assured her that he would be devastated, too, if something had happened to her. She had spent the last few days truly trying to be a real sincere, loving wife. She felt like, by the grace of God, she was making progress. If she detested fake people, then she needed to stop acting like that as well.

She had been very melancholy this morning, and her heart was mourning her beloved friend's state of mind. As the timer went off for the banana bread, she realized she had not even checked on Lady Jane in days! The Holy Spirit had been convicting her of all those secrets that she felt like she had to share with the world, even anonymously. She had shared a few of them through the years, but she did not think anyone took her seriously. It wasn't that she had blown them out of proportion, but she did obsess about them. She knew that she was somehow expecting vindication or validation by sharing them. Why on earth did she want to tell the whole world the sordid sin of her family?

This did not fit in with Philippians 4:8 or Ephesians 5:3, which said that none of those things should even be named among you. Here she was wanting to name sin and sinner. So much of this was supposedly already put under the blood of Jesus Christ, at least in her own heart; why was she dragging it back out to talk about it? She was obviously still obsessing over it. It was time to go clean that library and to help Lady Jane put all those things in the Crimson Vault.

She climbed the stairs determinedly to see what Lady Jane was up to today.

Entering the fairly quiet library, she stood for a moment letting the light from the windows bathe her in sunshine and to see if she could hear the bubbling fountain. Gathering herself to the task ahead, she looked at the Crimson door to her left, surprised to see books scattered across the walkway and the pile seriously smaller than she remembered.

"Lady Jane?" she called out.

Lady Jane had been sniffling all morning and feeling morose, she felt sadness that she could not explain, and she kept having sinking spells. When she heard Reba Jean's voice calling her from the entrance of the inner library, she wasn't sure she was up to the task that she knew had to be accomplished. Lady Jane came out sniffling with her head hung down; she might as well get it over with, if possible. Reba Jean took a long look at her and seemed to understand. She wrapped her arms around Lady Jane and hugged her close. Dipping the corner of her skirt in the fountain, she washed Lady Jane's face with the water from the Ancient One. Immediately, Lady Jane felt clean and refreshed and strengthened for the task ahead.

Reba Jean looked around and spotted the strange comparison chart nailed to the doorway and the ugly, green tapestry hanging near it. She curled her nose in disgust at it and looked to Lady Jane for an explanation. "Sid left it here for you," she explained to Reba Jean.

"Sid? Who is Sid?" she asked.

"Shhhhhh, he will hear you!" Lady Jane gasped in panic.

Reba Jean was not about to be distracted this time from learning what was going on in her library. She bade Lady Jane to tell her everything that had happened after she had left the other day. Reba Jean was appalled at the thought of some possible demonic force in her library wreaking havoc! She also knew that it was partially her fault. She had not put all those secrets and sins of the family in the Crimson Vault.

She reached out and took Lady Jane's hand, and together they began to gather the books and papers again. They did seem heavier than before, but together they carried them all back to the Crimson door of the vault. Reba Jean pulled an old iron key out of her pocket and unlocked the door to the vault. With much determination, they pushed in the pile of books. She mentally cataloged the titles to make sure they were all there: Asperger's Syndrome, Avoidant Personality Disorder,

Adultery, Abominations, Bitterness, Complaining, Deceit, Envy, Fornication, Frustration, Guilt, Hate, Jealousy… As she carefully kept the covers closed, these books need not be read or written in anymore. She looked around to see what might be lurking in the shadows trying to stay unnoticed and not dealt with properly. Ahh, there it was, the sequel to the book of abominations… That one needed to be completely gone from her library! Reba Jean knew that her library could only be free of these thoughts and deeds if she put it all under the blood of Christ.

She closed the strong door to the vault and laid the key down on the table by the Ancient One. Now, she needed to get rid of that ugly green tapestry that the Sid creature had left. She reached out to yank it down, and it seemed to sting her. She jumped back and looked around for something to use to dislodge it from its position. She found the long ladle that Lady Jane had used in the cauldron the other day. With care and slow movements, she knocked the tapestry down. What was this? The tapestry scuttled over and draped itself around the comparison chart that had been hung up. Lady Jane looked at Reba Jean to see what she would do with those.

Reba Jean read the chart quietly; it had her name versus other names that she was supposed to be like or aspire to emulate. After a minute of torturous musing, she walked back over to the Ancient One, flipping its gilded pages until she found the verse she was thinking about. "For we dare not make ourselves of the number, or compare ourselves with some that commend themselves…" She read this verse aloud in the direction of the comparison chart. She watched as the words of the Ancient One transformed the chart into something that was significantly different. It was an excerpt from the Beatitudes, and the tapestry with a shriek was transformed into a lovely, glittery, gossamer banner framing the beautiful words of the Ancient One.

Lady Jane looked in awe. What a relief to have the havoc from Sid changed into something that she knew the Overseer would approve. Lady Jane found a broom and started sweeping the hallway and setting the bookshelves in order. Things seemed bright and airy in there now with all those sins and weights taken care of and locked away. Reba Jean looked around the library and again noticed the weird dead ends in some of the corridors. She asked Lady Jane about it. "Those are paths that you started to take and then stopped and never proceeded further," she explained. Reba Jean thought for a minute and then flipped the pages of the Ancient One yet again. She opened to Job 23:10 and watched the words swirl out of the Book and onto the wall of one of those dead ends. Oh, what a way to make the library even more beautiful. Why hadn't she done this so many years ago? This Library of Secrets needed to be a library of serenity instead!

A feeling of peace and tranquility descended upon them both as they flipped through the pages of the Ancient One, reading its precious words.

This is the day which the Lord hath made, we will rejoice and be glad in it, they thought. Reba Jean drew Lady Jane down to the floor under the shelter of the Ancient One and asked her the burning questions that she had been pondering for days now.

"Lady Jane, who are you?" she wondered aloud.

"Reba Jean, I am your inner child, the voice in your head, I am your conscience, that is put here to help you keep your thoughts. I am supposed to bring order to chaos and help you remember who you are," she explained the best she could.

"So... you are part of me?" puzzled Reba Jean. "Then... who is Sid?"

With a puff of sulfurous smoke, a charming, devilishly handsome man-like creature appeared behind them. "You rang?" he chuckled. Doffing his top hat and swishing the tails of a tuxedo, he bowed low over Reba Jean's hand and kissed it. "I am Sid, at your service; pleased to meet you, Milady. It's good to have another beautiful lady here besides the ever-lovely Lady Jane. What have you done to this place? Well, we can fix it back up again, I'm sure. I thought I had left it looking much better than this the last time I was here," he rubbed his hands in anticipation.

Reba Jean looked at this Sid creature in a bit of shock and amazement. Something felt off about him. This was her library; she now knew who Lady Jane was, but who was Sid? Reba Jean looked around for something to explain all this in a logical sense. She noticed that Sid was standing in front of the Ancient One like he was trying to hide it from view. In a daze, she watched him wave his hand, and the long-handled spoon that Lady Jane had discarded picked up some smelly black ooze and dribbled it into the fountain.

"Stop!" Reba Jean yelled. "Who do you think you are, and why are you here?"

"Why, Milady, don't get so excited; you invited me here," Sid brushed off her order. Reba Jean lowered her brow in frustration and wondered how to get rid of this creature before he undid everything they had worked on so hard this morning.

She glanced up at the misty tendrils of muse and had an idea. She watched as the tendrils poised in readiness for her thought. She thought and thought some more and watched as the tendrils wrapped themselves around Sid and pulled him into an open page of a waiting book. Maybe she could close him into a book and drop him into a vault somewhere! Sid flicked off the tendrils with a bit of annoyance and touched the page of the book, turning it to ash. He decided to exert his authority; Reba Jean needed to know that he belonged here even more than Lady Jane did. Sid twirled his long, tapered finger and burned a saying into the wall. The smell was enough to make Lady Jane and Reba Jean choke and cough.

What could they do? Sid seemed to have all the power in the library right now. The Ancient One was silent, the fountain didn't seem to be as bubbly, and the air smelled of burning flesh. Sid looked at the girls with a gleam in his eyes. Yes, girls, he thought; he would whittle them down to the little, blubbering schoolgirls that he knew they really were. He raked his claw-like fingers down the side of a bookcase, and it screeched like fingernails on a chalkboard. Oh, this was going to be so much fun, at least to Sid.

Reba Jean knew she needed help, Lady Jane looked powerless, and Sid was just running amok in the library, writing on walls and cackling with devilish glee. She turned to Lady Jane and whispered… "I will be right back, I promise; I need to clear my thoughts and pray!"

Lady Jane panicked at the thought of once again being left along with the powerful Sid, who just seemed to bring mayhem and destruction to everything in his reach. Lady Jane understood the need to talk to Lord Rabboni, but why couldn't she do that here?

Lady Jane tried to slip away unnoticed to hide until Reba Jean told her it was safe again. Sid caught her sidling away and reached out with a tentacle-like arm and grabbed her in his tight, painful grip. "NO, Milady! You are mine now," he bellowed in a commanding tone. Lady Jane crumpled in his grasp and started sobbing like a little girl.

Reba Jean ran out of the library, down the stairs, and fell to her knees in the living room. She cried out to the Lord for help. What was going on in the library, and how could she stop it? As she cried out to the Lord, the answer came to her.

The Holy Spirit reminded her that she was to be wearing the helmet of Salvation and to use the Sword of the Spirit to fight off the fiery darts of the wicked. Where was her suit of armor? Where was her shield of faith? She could not defeat the armies of the wicked one if she wasn't prepared for battle. She would lose her mind if she didn't make use of the defense that the Lord had provided her. She cried as she prayed, and the Lord brought the words of Scripture to her mind. Thoughts of peace to give her an expected end if she only obeyed Him at His Word.

With hope renewed and help on her side, she ran up the stairs to the library again. She rushed into the room and flipped open the Ancient One to the right page. Touching the page, she watched a suit of armor form in front of her, along with a shield and a large, fierce-looking sharp sword. Before Sid could even fathom what was happening, the Sword came after him, forcing him to release Lady Jane from his wicked grasp. Lady Jane collapsed in a heap, but the Sword wasn't finished. It chased Sid all the way to the door and kicked him out of the library altogether! Wow, what a relief to know that they were free of Sid, at least for now.

Reba Jean helped Lady Jane up and checked her for wounds or broken bones. They both ran to the fountain, which was bubbling along merrily again, and refreshed themselves in its cleansing water. Lady Jane looked at Reba Jean in awe in her beautiful suit of armor and shield. The Sword had come to rest at her side for a minute. The Sword was very much alive and seemed to have its own orders to follow.

The ladies looked around at the walls full of black graffiti and knew they needed to cover or wash away those vile words. Flipping the pages of the Ancient One to various passages, they watched the golden dust motes turn into beautiful calligraphy covering the burned words with lovely, just, true words straight from Lord Rabboni Himself.

Reba Jean wondered how often Sid ran rampant in the library. She did not want to speak her thought aloud in case he thought it was an invitation to return. She had a feeling he wasn't finished with her yet. She looked down at her armor and knew she needed to get used to wearing it or else the next episode might end in the total destruction of the library.

After a bit more cleaning and organizing and soaking in the hymns, they could finally both hear through the sound system; they sat back and just took a few minutes to daydream. The misty tendrils of muse drew lovely pictures in open book pages and entertained them with peaceful mental pictures drawn in fluffy clouds and floating butterflies. Lady Jane sighed; what a huge difference this was. Maybe having Reba Jean here was a very good thing, especially in that suit of armor. She glanced at the Sword that stood propped on the table holding the Ancient One and hoped it would stay close to protect her forever.

Reba Jean seemed to come out of her sweet daydream; the books gently closed as the tendrils withdrew back into the overhead mist. She knew it was time to leave the library in peace and get back to reality. She needed to ask the Lord about Sid, but she didn't want to do it anywhere near the library. He seemed to have too much familiarity with her library, and that disturbed her more than she knew how to express. She hugged Lady Jane and tried to assure her that the rest of her day, hopefully, would be more peaceful. She knew, though, that if Lady Jane was truly going to be at peace, then she needed to keep her thoughts aligned with Philippians 4:8.

She left Lady Jane and went down to the kitchen to see what she should eat for lunch. She still had yard work to do. Reba Jean was wondering what she should write about now that all the secrets had been locked away in the Crimson Vault. Maybe she should just write about the library and its design and purpose, not what she had turned it into. Sid needed to be banished forever somehow from that special place. She had a feeling it was her fault that he was allowed to have free access to it.

Reba Jean pondered everything that had happened in just a short amount of time that morning. She knew that time seemed to run differently in the library than it did in her everyday life. She looked around as if coming out of a stupor and heard the song "Holy, Holy, Holy" begin to play on the sound system. *Thoughts of peace to give me an expected end,* she thought to herself.

Who was Sid, and how could she get rid of him? That would be her next mission, and she wasn't sure she really wanted to know the answer. What if Sid was also a part of herself, like Lady Jane? Did she have alter-egos, split personalities, or was it something different? Reba Jean tried to stop thinking about it all; it was time to get some yard work finished and go about her daily routine. She had to shake off the effect the library had on her, or she would never get anything finished.

Chapter 6

Everything was so hazy in the library the next morning. Lady Jane felt like she was moving in slow motion and getting nowhere. She tried to clean up some more and organize the shelves after all those books had been stored in the Crimson Vault. She stood still and tried to gather her thoughts. Her night hadn't been too bad, for once. At least what she could remember of it, she mused. A book skittered across the floor in front of her, misty tendrils dipped down to write, only to ascend again into the cloud overhead. She saw this happening all around the library as she meandered along the aisles. She needed to find a way to make the books put themselves back on the shelves when they weren't being written in. She tripped over another book that plopped at her feet that was struggling to open its pages. What was Reba Jean doing? The cloud of mist descended closer to Lady Jane's head, and tendrils wrapped themselves all around her, making it even harder to see or move. She felt too groggy to even care or panic. There was no music playing through the sound system; the windows seemed gray today, with no sunlight filtering down into the library.

She heard the faint whir of electronics from Sir Theo's library. Ahhh, Sir Theo was home today. She slipped over and peeked into his strange library. She had been so encouraged the last time she looked in to see that he had his own electronic version of the Ancient One and was searching through the heavenly prophecies. He was immersed in his video escape from reality. She envied him sometimes but was so used to her own library home that she didn't think she wanted to live in his.

Unbeknownst to her, as she was lingering in the doorway of Sir Theo's library, Sid slithered into the library behind her. He surveyed the hazy mist, the scattered books, the random artifacts flying off walls and shelves, and cackled under his breath. He loved days like this in the library. The ladies couldn't string a single thought together to save their lives. He had not actually orchestrated this but used it to his advantage every time that he could.

He glanced over to the table holding the Ancient One and saw the gleaming sword that had chased him from the library earlier leaning against it. His glowing eyes skimmed over the iron key sitting there on the old, rugged wood. He started to look away, then swung his evil gaze back to the key. "What was this?" he pondered. It must go to one of these locked vaults or a locked chest. This surely could come in handy. He dripped some black ooze around the key, forming a mold of the key. With a touch of his finger, the ooze hardened into a hard tar mold of the iron key. Slipping the mold into his cloak, he looked around to see where Lady Jane was. She was standing in the archway leading to Sir Theo's library. Sid contemplated if he should stir up some strife or discord between them. He had done it so many times; he was amazed at how very easy it was—just a twist of a word or tone could set them both off into a disagreement. He didn't mind when they apologized or tried to work it out. He knew he could just do it all over again.

He fingered the mold of the key and decided to come back another time to try all the locks. He knew he couldn't get into some places, or at least he didn't think he could. With this copy of the iron key in his possession, however, maybe all that would change. The ladies would never know he had been here, especially with all this haze around. He had a feeling he knew what had happened to cause such a gloomy atmosphere here in the library. He cackled again softly and slipped away to his realm.

Reba Jean was so scatterbrained this morning. She had slept pretty well, thanks to the sleeping draught she had taken. She always hated how it made her feel the next day. She didn't know what drugs did to a person, but that cherry-flavored cold medicine was bad enough.

Her husband was home for the day, and all was quiet for now. She had done housework, put in some laundry, and commissioned some keepsakes to be made for her grieving friend's family. She was productive but just couldn't gather her thoughts together to go see Lady Jane.

Not realizing, yet again, that her reality always affected the library, she went about trying to write some more in her book. Reba Jean had never tried to write while she was groggy or while her husband was home. She heard the dryer buzzer go off, so saving her last few paragraphs, she flitted off to check on the laundry. She needed to remember that today was Wednesday, and she had church tonight. It wasn't even noon, and here she was, ready for a nap. It was probably the aftereffects of the cold medicine. What was she doing? Oh, yeah, she was going to take care of the laundry. *This was getting crazy*, she thought to herself. *I can't even remember what I was just thinking!*

She took care of the laundry, hoping it would no longer be a distraction nagging at her while she worked on her novel. What was the use of typing today if she was so distracted by every little thing? Thinking back on her previous adventures in the library, she remembered a quote she had seen. *An empty mind is a noisy mind* or something to that effect. She did not think that was completely accurate. Her mind was chock full and very noisy. An empty mind might echo, but hers definitely seemed to be hardly ever quiet.

Reba Jean's eyes wandered over to her tablet, and she scrolled through social media looking for other stuff she could use in her research for her book. It was scary how social media seemed to read her mind. It felt almost creepy that what she was thinking would show up on her feed. She hoped it was God orchestrating it to help her. She needed to spend less time watching television or scrolling through posts. She knew that what she watched or listened to was affecting her life. She missed the hymns playing on the sound system; they were so soothing and quiet. It even put the cats in a calmer mood, she had noticed.

Her husband hated silence, and she realized that sometimes she did as well. Her mind was far from quiet; she knew she needed to work on that, somehow.

Another hot flash came over her; she turned on the fan to cool her flushed skin. It was hard to think of anything significant during a hot flash. Her fingers stopped typing, and she tried to breathe through the episode. Now, she was distracted and getting hungry; she would never string two sentences together at this rate. Her husband being home was a real distraction, and he wasn't even talking to her at the moment. "Ugh, stuff and nonsense," she muttered to herself.

The hot flash dissipated, and she shivered from the breeze of the fan. Well, obviously, she would need to eat something. Why was every little thing such a hindrance today? She could still feel the effects of the cold medicine in her system. It lasted all the next day, usually. She had taken that into consideration but desperately wanted to sleep all night for once. Maybe, she wasn't supposed to write today? Was there something else she should be doing instead?

Reba Jean thought through her list of chores, mentally checking them off by priority. She had already taken care of the memorials and had taken care of her husband. Maybe she needed to check on him again. She did spoil him, but it made her life easier if he wasn't stomping around looking for things, making messes, and complaining. His moods always affected hers, especially when he was grumpy or angry. She had told him many times to be careful as she was very much an empath. Getting up from her chair, she went to check on him. Maybe, he was trying to mentally let her know he needed something.

Odd, his office door had been mostly shut; that was rare. He had his headphones on, playing his game, though, so he wasn't doing anything secretive. She removed his lunch plate and checked his coffee and sweet tea, ensuring they did not need to be refilled yet. She mused over the nearly closed door. That brought back memories she did not want to resurrect right now. She had to trust him; he had been so good the last sixteen years. It was scary, though, how the least little thing like a nearly closed door would invoke such a sense of suspicion in her mind. She thought about all the things she had locked in the Crimson Vault yesterday and realized that this was one of them that she had not seen in the pile. She would need to get upstairs to the library and find that missing book. It did not need to be creeping around the library wreaking havoc.

Reba Jean knew she needed to check on Lady Jane anyway. Why did she once again feel so reluctant? Was it the lethargy from the cold medicine? Was it a sense of apathy or laziness?

Lady Jane felt really tired; she withdrew from Sir Theo's library entrance and went to her chaise lounge to rest. She barely noticed what the books and misty tendrils were doing. She just wanted to not have to do anything for a few minutes. Could she actually go to sleep? Lady Jane had tried sleeping before, but it seemed that only happened when Reba Jean was under anesthesia. Right, twice in her whole life had she been asleep. She rubbed her sleepy eyes and listened to the muted sounds of books dropping and keys clacking away from two keyboards.

She glanced at the Ancient One, but it too was quiet. Drifting off into a daze, she twirled her finger through a ringlet and hoped for a lazy day.

Hearing a constant plopping in one of the aisles, she glanced to see a book thumping up and down like it was stuck in a loop. It couldn't open, and it couldn't get back on the shelf. Whatever could be the problem? Lady Jane did not want to investigate, she did not want to help the book, and she did NOT want any sort of excitement. She buried her tired face into her hands and tried to block out all the stuff she knew she should be doing.

Reba Jean listened to her stomach growl but just could not think of what to eat for lunch. She had gained weight over the past two days even with all the yard work. This weight struggle had become a real frustration, and she had no answers.

For all she knew, sitting and typing was making her gain weight. She knew this was temporary, though. Once she sent the book to the publishers, she would need to find other things to do. The book was becoming such a huge part of her life right now. She would think of plot twists and see material that needed to be added to it. What would life be like when the book was finished? Maybe, she was meant to write a series? She could call them the Lady Jane Chronicles or something.

What would Lady Jane think if she had a whole series of books written in her honor?

Mardie had told her yesterday by text how proud she was of her for writing a book. She, too, thought it was a gift from God since it seemed to be just flowing so easily out of her. Reba Jean needed to be so careful not to get filled with pride. If this book was any good, it was because God wanted it to be, not any sort of talent for word usage of hers.

Enough of this, she thought; it was just time to eat something, even if it was a protein shake. She had been hoping to start fasting for spiritual renewal, but she couldn't even fast to lose weight. She poured herself some juice and more water and then checked on her husband, who was chatting with a gaming partner. Her tablet dinged with a message, and she saw it was her grieving friend. She was sharing videos of her father singing in church. *Surrounded by so great a cloud of witnesses, let us run the race with patience…* thought Reba Jean.

A flurry of messages back and forth between different groups kept Reba Jean occupied for a little while. She still hadn't eaten lunch and really had no clue what she was going to find palatable.

Reba Jean wandered aimlessly around her kitchen, wondering what to eat; nothing really sounded good. She rubbed her aching wrists and mused about getting old. Imagine having arthritis at her age already. She sat back down in front of the keyboard and rubbed her hands over her face. She was still lethargic and a bit melancholy, knowing that her dear friend was suffering such a devastating heartache. She could really only pray for her and be there for her as much as possible.

Reba Jean doubted that she would have the same reaction to any of her parents passing away, though. She knew she would be secretly relieved when they were gone. She felt guilt over feeling that way and guilt that things hadn't improved after all these years. She doubted she would ever have a sense of closure or answers to the "why" of all her childhood.

She remembered the quote she had read earlier last week. *Our circumstances form us, but our choices define us.* She felt that was so profound and so relevant in her life.

Her brain was so distracted listening to her husband's gaming chatter, reading messages from a grieving friend, strange bird noises coming from the other part of the house, and her growling stomach. Her husband's chatter got louder, and she just could not concentrate. She had not even gone to the library or checked on Lady Jane. She barely even thought about needing to deal with that missing book or figuring out who Sid was. All she knew was that she needed to clear her head before she could tackle anything important. She also anticipated that she would have to deal with something monumental; isn't that what usually happened when she wasn't ready for it?

She stopped to listen to her husband and shook her head for a few seconds. She still couldn't even seem to think; everything was all sludge-y in her mind.

Getting up to check on her husband, she got a few caresses from him and then went to refill his coffee. Shivering in the kitchen, she mused over nothing in particular. She could just go sit in front of the television, cuddle up in a soft blanket, and watch some mindless program. It seemed that every time she wanted to stop watching tv so much or being on social media, something would pull her back in, and there she would be, filling her mind with mostly useless stuff.

Reba Jean had started a group chat with the mourning family, and it began filling up with memories of their lost loved one. She felt like maybe she was part of an anchor that kept them from losing their minds over this heartbreak.

She remembered the devastation she had suffered when her beloved mother-in-love had been suddenly taken from this world. She had been the strong one, though, so that all the others could fall apart. She had been resentful of that often enough, like she wasn't allowed to grieve or fall apart. She wasn't allowed to be angry or throw temper tantrums either. It was all right for others, but somehow, she was never supposed to do that. She wasn't sure why she was held to some other standard than everyone else was. The thoughts of that frustration welled up inside of her anew.

Sitting with her chin in her hands, she watched the pictures get uploaded into the group chat. If this was therapeutic for them, let it happen. They had a long road ahead of them; she knew that from years of experience. Setting aside thoughts of the library, Lady Jane, missing books, and her own need to get things sorted out, she wandered back into the kitchen, craving all the foods she shouldn't eat. She shivered again as the furnace kicked on; well, at least it wasn't all in her head; maybe it was actually chilly in the house.

Looking through the pictures they had posted in memory, she had a sense that they would pull through this. She knew if they let the Lord be their help, they would make it. She heard her husband sharing a funny story about one of his best friends, and she realized that everyone's lives are built from memories.

She continued to scroll mindlessly through social media until a quote by a well-known missionary popped up in her stream. It spoke of the difficulty of waiting on God and doing it silently until God was ready to reveal His answer. Thinking about that for a few minutes, she felt like she needed to remember that. Silence did not have to be loud; it needed to be a time of waiting on God, serving Him, and letting Him control the situations. What did she feel most deeply about? It was obvious by whatever her strongest reactions were when the topic was broached. Her family, her childhood, her relationship with her husband, these things needed to be talked over thoroughly with her Heavenly Father.

She saw another post that she thought was also relevant to her right now. It stated *When people praise you, don't let it go to your head; when they criticize you, don't let it go to your heart.*

Realizing that she still hadn't eaten, she wondered if maybe the distraction of everything and nothing was a tool she could use to help her fast. Now, there was a thought. If she wasted enough time, maybe it would keep her from eating anything or everything. *Does Lady Jane eat?* now there was an interesting thought. She would have to ask her that question the next time she was with her in the library. She really hoped it wasn't a diet of bookworms or wood mites or some other food for thought.

Later that day, before church, Reba Jean sat down to write a bit more in her book. She had watched some mind-numbing television, puttered some more with the memorial designs, made supper, and tried not to overthink things. She wondered how much of her obsessiveness affected her life and how she got along with people. Sometimes she was very content, and other times she was so uncomfortable with everything. Reba Jean laughed at herself; who was she fooling; she was uncomfortable in her own skin. She was so much aware of nearly every molecule in her body. That may be a symptom of the autistic gene she carried within her. She knew the avoidant personality disorder came from living with someone who had undiagnosed Asperger's Syndrome. She had asked God many agonizing times why she had been chosen to be in this particular family. It seemed that God wanted her to use her pain and her longings to help others who felt the same way she did. Her Heavenly Father made no mistakes, and He continued to be her best Friend through all these years. All the other situations that had been written down in the books in the library and then locked in the Crimson Vault were choices that she or others had made that affected their whole lives. She knew that by putting them under the blood of Jesus Christ, she was surrendering the effect they had on her personally. Dwelling on them did not change them, only changed her into a very miserable person.

A few years ago, she had personally sought a closer walk with the Lord and really wanted to glean from His Precious Word. She wanted real personal time with God every day. She had to move her prayer closet to different locations sometimes, and now that she was home every day, she looked forward to no more excuses for having a real prayer life again. She had been convicted of her thought life for a long time now and really worked at keeping it in alignment with Philippians 4:8. However, she often found that this was harder for her to do with her past or even her present coming up to trip her. Reba Jean knew that she could have a better thought life if she wanted to and that it would improve her overall life. She often felt like she was a spectator, not a participator, detached and withdrawn. Whether this was just her way of coping or hiding from dealing with people and situations, she wasn't sure. All she knew was that she wanted the abundant life that God had for her, and she wondered if she was keeping Him from pouring these blessings all over her because she was critical and insecure.

Checking the clock, she realized that she probably needed to wait to visit the library until tomorrow. She hoped that Lady Jane could keep things running up there in a well-functioning manner. She would just have to deal with that Sid creature and the Library of Secrets another time. Church was just an hour away, and she needed to look presentable for the House of God. She needed to stop being so distracted and start praying for the service tonight. Someone might be there that needed Jesus, and she did not want the service hindered by her attitude or restlessness. That was another thing she needed to work on again. Enjoying church like she used to; she wasn't sure when she started getting uncomfortable, probably during the time of upheaval with class regroupings, seating changes, people leaving, and people just being people.

People were such strange creatures, but she was one of them. Who set the standard for "normal" anyways? There she was getting all snarky again. Trying to remember that her life was to be all about living for Jesus, Reba Jean slunk off to get ready for the mid-week prayer service. Service, yes, it was about serving the Lord, and then she could serve others. "How may I serve You today, Lord?" she breathed in silent prayer as she got ready for church.

It was well into the next morning before Reba Jean sat back down to work on her book. She pondered over all her various rabbit trail-like thoughts from the night before. Church had been good, but she still felt detached. She wasn't really close to many of the members there, but that was also her choosing. She found them to be on a completely different level than she was. That was okay, she had a few close friends, and that was all she could keep up with. She had joked with her husband about him being impressed if her book was actually published. He laughed about it being a best seller, and she replied that it would be another one that he had never read. He would have to listen to it read to him instead. He laughed at their inside joke of her reading voice putting its listeners to sleep. She really hoped her book wasn't boring and what someone used to fall asleep.

Reba Jean knew she was being insecure again; it came so naturally to her after all these years of not measuring up. Her mind rambled around aimlessly as she watched the rain outside and listened to the coffee pot percolating away. It might be the weather or the upcoming funeral that had her all melancholy today. A phrase from a song in church last night ran through her mind… a wall of prayer to keep out the devil. Her mind grasped onto that thought, and she knew that besides the missing book in that library, she needed to build a wall of prayer to keep Satan and his minions out of her inner thoughts!

Something clearly needed to be done about Sid, that was for sure. Reba Jean knew it was time to check on the library and to make sure Lady Jane was able to do her tasks without Sid bothering her or other mayhem that seemed to abound. She still hadn't totally grasped that a lot of the mayhem was her own fault personally. She was too distracted by the mayhem to understand it.

Lady Jane heard the soothing sounds of the orchestrated hymns playing through the sound system as she puttered around picking up strewn books and papers from yesterday. She knew that sooner than later, she would have to let Reba Jean see the real truth of the library. She knew that Reba Jean still thought that Lady Jane was the one making the messes every day. Time would come when that would need to be dealt with, although today probably would not be that day. She did not think Reba Jean was ready for that part of the library business.

Hearing the slow tread of footsteps on the staircase to the library, she straightened her hair and skirts and glanced around to see how the library might look from Reba Jean's viewpoint. Oh well, no use hiding the dishevelment.

The chime over the door tinkled softly as Reba Jean entered the atrium of the main level of the library. She paused and listened to the soothing sounds of the hymns playing through the sound system. She saw the Crimson Door off to the left was locked tight. That was a comforting thought, and then she felt for the key in her pocket. It wasn't there! She could not lose that key! Her eyes widened in alarm, and she looked around the remains of the mess in the library. The misty tendrils were looking more like Spanish moss hanging around today. Books were half opened or suspended in midair. She opened her mouth and then closed it. Where was that old iron key?

Ahh, there it was on the rugged wooden table by the Ancient One. She breathed a huge sigh of relief and went to retrieve it before it got lost. She noticed it felt slick and oily as she picked it up. A few drops of black ooze were on the table next to it. She just believed that the Ancient One had protected it from evil, and she pocketed the key in her skirt. Lady Jane was watching her silently and just seemed a bit detached today.

Reba Jean turned to Lady Jane and reached out a timid hand to her. Lady Jane eyed her outstretched hand, and a myriad of expressions flitted across her features. Reba Jean thought Lady Jane was looking more tired than anything else. She gently grasped her hand in hers and drew her to the settee. They sat in an odd silence, surveying the mess still hovering around the library. Reba Jean puzzled to herself, and as a misty tendril dropped down to write in a book, it was like the light was slowly dawning. The misty tendril began writing Reba Jean's thoughts down on the open page in the book. Reba Jean stood up and grabbed the book as she checked for a title. It read "Mind Games and other Puzzles." She clapped the book shut and put it back on the shelf. Her eyes widened as she caught sight of the titles around it. "Mindless Trivia," "Manipulation," and another "Malicious Intent."

That word "intent" reminded her of a verse from the Ancient One, and she ran over to look it up. It was about the Golden Sword that was resting against the table. She picked up the Sword, and as she looked at it, the verse swirled its golden words around the two-edged blades. It was a discerner of the thoughts and intents of the heart. She knew that her mind was the gateway to her heart. Her eyes glanced at the porous walls that seemed to allow everything in as if it was a thin transparent membrane. Still holding the Sword, she looked at Lady Jane and tried to comprehend it all.

Lady Jane waited to see if she would grasp the whole truth of the library. She felt suspended in time as she watched Reba Jean look around the main level of the library. She noticed when Reba Jean got another almost wild expression on her face and started rummaging through the wooden chests.

"Lady Jane!" sounded through the library in an urgent whisper. Reba Jean whispered in Lady Jane's ear. She was looking for the book that had not been put in the Crimson Vault the other day. Lady Jane jerked back as if scorched by her touch. She had forgotten about that book and had hoped never to see it again. Had Sid kicked it out of sight? Had it even been in the pile in the first place?

Maybe it was in Sir Theo's library, as it had originated from his library to begin with. They tiptoed over the archway leading to his quiet library. No, Sir Theo had reassured her that that particular topic was no longer an ongoing issue or threat since he had surrendered to King Abba and Lord Rabboni years earlier. If the book was still in the library, then it was Reba Jean's book now and needed to be dealt with accordingly. Reba Jean couldn't find it in the chest downstairs or on any of the bookshelves. She glanced around and saw a winding staircase up to another level of the library. Climbing it in a hasty stumble, she reached a part of the library she had not noticed in her earlier visits. It was dusty up here, full of cobwebs and a moldy stench permeated the stale air. Lady Jane had reluctantly followed her. There were more wooden chests up here, and then she saw a faint glow come from under a door that she had barely noticed. She tried the doorknob, and it swung open with very little resistance. She peeked inside, and there was Sid! He had all sorts of lurid pictures, books opened, and sordid images swirled around his head.

Reba Jean gasped and yet couldn't seem to look away. Was this Sid's room? Why did he have a room in HER library?! She looked down and realized she still had the Sword of truth in her hand. She brandished the Sword around the room and at Sid. Immediately, the images shrunk back into their books; Sid howled in anger and lunged at her. She dodged his attack, swung the Sword at him, and chased him down the stairs. Tossing the key to Lady Jane, she commanded her to lock that room up tight! No one needed to see that nasty place ever again!

Sid ran howling from the library but cackled to himself as he left. Those silly women had no clue whom they were dealing with; why he had the key to the library and that room and knew he could torment them any time he pleased.

He knew that even though Lady Jane had locked the room, it was more symbolic than anything else. They had not cleaned out the contents of the room or put it in the Crimson Vault. He would sneak back in later and unlock that little speakeasy of a room.

The two women collapsed in a heap until Reba Jean got a determined look on her face and pulled Lady Jane up to her feet. "We need to start here at the front door," she stated, "and start a thorough cleaning today. This place is in such disarray."

Together, they organized books and shooed away any misty musings that wanted to scribble, draw, or record. Sweeping hallways, moving boxes, and re-cataloging titles kept them busy for most of the day. Eyeing some of the hatboxes that they had uncovered in their task, Reba Jean knew she had more memories to sort and store away. Memories could be a dangerous thing; she decided to leave the boxes closed—for now.

Lady Jane was glad to have help organizing and cleaning for once. It seemed such an arduous task all by herself every day. These were all of Reba Jean's things anyway; she should be the one to clean up. Lady Jane realized that she actually hoped Reba Jean would take full charge of the library and put her out of a job!

A bit taken aback by this truth, she nonetheless realized it needed to happen. Lord Rabboni would expect Reba Jean to take responsibility once she realized the truth of the library. Lady Jane knew that someday she might just be a figment of imagination or a faint memory, and that was how it should be.

With renewed determination, Lady Jane organized books and research materials on another shelf. She had been lazy lately, and that needed to stop. If the Overseer came for inspection, she needed to show Him that she was doing her very best to obey Him.

Reba Jean wasn't really aware of what Lady Jane was silently thinking, but she saw her begin to work harder, and soon the library was looking very organized and clean. Lady Jane gave her back the key, and together they promised each other that they would take better care of this special place.

Reba Jean surveyed the library; it felt like a calm oasis right now, and she closed her eyes and listened to the rain outside and the beautiful strands of music. A misty tendril touched her face, and she glanced to see what it would do. Almost timidly, it danced toward a book laying in the corner. The book opened its pages, and out danced beautiful blue butterflies. Lady Jane realized she had held her breath through all this and exhaled in relief. The blue butterflies danced around the ceiling of the library. Reba Jean loved blue butterflies and decided they would not bring any harm to their efforts to clean and organize.

Lady Jane started giggling; she loved having moments of joy and peace descend in this place. It seemed to be so chaotic more often than not. The blue butterflies were such a happy sight to behold. She wondered if Lady Constance ever had blue butterflies in her library. What would Lady Matilda think of this? Was it too fanciful and shallow, or was it just a necessary balm to the chaos that had ensued the last few weeks?

Reba Jean smiled softly as she watched Lady Jane relax and giggle like a little schoolgirl. She decided that they had accomplished a lot for the day, and it would be nice to leave on a good note. She bid Lady Jane a fond fare-thee-well, and after a loving hug, she exited the library.

She touched the key in her pocket and assured herself that all was safe in the library once again. She totally forgot that the contents of that disgusting room would never be safe unless it was put away once and forever in the Crimson Vault. Little did she yet realize how much danger she and Lady Jane were still going to experience. Even though she had chased Sid away, she had not built a wall of prayer to keep him out.

Feeling a false sense of security, Reba Jean wandered back down to the living room. Picking up her tablet, she decided to scroll through social media instead of watching mindless television. She loved the hymns playing, and they kept her thoughts calm. Surely, that was a good thing. Besides, she reasoned, she probably needed more research for her book. She needed food for thought, so to speak.

Lady Jane felt a great calm descend on her, yet she felt like they had much unfinished business that still needed attention in this library of theirs. She was glad Sid was gone, at least for now. She was so used to having him around creating chaos or adding to Reba Jean's chaos that she was beginning to think that it was normal. The misty tendrils were quiet for the moment, and all the books stayed closed in their positions. Wow, that was also rare; usually, they were flying around the rooms and off their shelves, tripping her up or making her duck to avoid getting whacked by one. She made her way back to her boudoir and sat down to await whatever would happen next. They had made great headway today; she felt very pleased with their efforts. The Overseer ought to be pleased with her progress.

Reba Jean paused almost in a daze but wasn't really thinking. This rarely happened as her brain was always busy, even with random musings. The ticking of the clock was the only other sound besides the rain and music. She had most of her housework done, and she could probably procrastinate on the rest. She was really good at procrastination. She would lie to herself and call it time management and prioritizing. It was laziness and apathy at the heart of it. The hymn currently playing was well known, and yet, she just couldn't seem to recall the words, as she seemed lost in thought, yet not really thinking of anything. Forcing herself to pay attention to the music, she listened to the next song, and soon the words started playing in her memory. That was better; maybe she wasn't losing her mind just yet.

Lady Jane looked up to see music notes and lyrics descend from the mist and swirl around the Ancient One in worship and praise. She clapped her hands softly in delight and closed her eyes to soak in the atmosphere of worship that seemed to descend in the library. *Oh! This is how it really should be*, she thought to herself. Reba Jean seemed to be in a good place mentally right now when she was worshipping Lord Rabboni and King Abba.

"How Great Thou Art" was playing through the sound system, and both women closed their eyes and soaked in the timeless words of worship and praise to their Creator God. All time and thought were suspended as Reba Jean felt her heart humble itself before the Lord. *Then sings my soul, my Savior God to Thee, how great Thou art,* she sang in her heart to the Lord. Thoughts of Sid and Lady Jane and the library receded as she just focused on her Savior and what He had done for her by saving her from her sin. Her heart lifted up on sweet serenity to the One Who had made her.

Sid thought this might be a good time to slip back into the library, as both women were otherwise occupied. He went to the door, but the sweet odor of praise and prayer repulsed him. "Ugh!" He growled. He despised that sweet savor and the odors of saints praying. The doorknob would not turn under his fingers, and he was a bit surprised. He had taken for granted how easy it had been to usually just waltz in like he owned the place. He fingered the key that he had copied from the other day. He could be patient; his room was still there waiting for him—he was sure.

Reba Jean continued to soak the hymns of old into her very heart and soul. Lady Jane leaned back against the rugged wooden stand holding the Ancient One and closed her eyes in peace. "I need Thee, Oh I need Thee, every hour I need thee" filtered through the golden dust motes and caressed her weary form.

Shaking herself from her reverie, Reba Jean knew she needed to finish her housework and get back to reality of sorts. This book might write itself if it was in the library, but here in the kitchen, it required someone actually typing on the keys and making sense of the jumble of words and information.

She knew she would still have to deal with Sid; she had a niggling suspicion that their battles were not over with. She couldn't see the golden Sword down here, but she had her Bible open next to her, and that was the same thing. Glancing at the verse she had seen upstairs in the library, she thanked

God for that gleaming golden Sword of Truth which was the Word of God.

Feeling energized, she decided to force herself to finish cleaning the house before she worked on making lunch. No time like the present, she knew. The house did not clean itself, and neither did the library. That thought seemed to stick out at her for a moment, but she didn't grasp the full impact of it.

While she was scrubbing the floors in the bathroom, she realized that she had not realized how deep down dirty they were until she started removing the layers. The counter had set in stains that she thought might never come out. Fortunately, she found that a combination of strong chemicals released the stains, and she was able to remove them. She compared the bathroom cleaning to the task that she knew needed to be done in the library still. It needed a deep cleaning. She probably had more books that needed to be closed shut, never to be reopened. She needed to get that cloud of mist under control, and she tried to figure out what to do with that Sid character. Lady Jane seemed unable to do anything about him. She would need to find a cleansing agent of some sort to remove all the deep stains embedded and ground into the very fiber and framework of the library. She was not up to the task alone; she knew that.

Reba Jean decided that she really needed to finish the tour of the library that week and evaluate what needed to be done to get it more manageable for her and Lady Jane to take care of. Still not sure how to really get rid of Sid, she shelved that thought for another day. She knew she had a wall of prayer to build, but why did it seem not as urgent as she had thought before?

Sid heard these thoughts and stirred his finger lazily around in a circle on the door to the library. He did not necessarily need to get into the library; he could just keep her from going in there. He continued to swirl a lazy finger of apathy around, keeping Reba Jean from feeling like continuing her tasks.

Lady Jane, meanwhile, leaned back in a daydream, never realizing that Sid was just outside the door. She might be very familiar with him, and he seemed to think he owned her body and soul, but she was still very uncomfortable around him and always felt terror or at least unease when he was around. Scratching a sudden itch, she still didn't realize how close he was to her in her lazy stupor.

Sid really did want back in the library, but he saw how effective just his presence at the door was having on both women. The power and control he exerted over them made him shrug off the memory of the golden Sword or the dusty Ancient One that often got the best of him. He knew the women did not understand the true power they wielded, and that lack of knowledge comforted him. He dripped some black ooze on the library door and swirled his finger in it forming a faint pentagram. He blew his hot breath on it and watched it harden and blacken on the door. This was his library; he would banish that Ancient One and the golden Sword, and Lady Jane and Reba Jean would be his slaves. That supposedly locked room upstairs would be expanded, and all those lurid creatures would be able to cavort through the whole library. Maybe he would get them to slither back into that Sir Theo's library. He doubted that would be hard to accomplish. Men were designed to want the flesh and carnality of his world.

Sid was well pleased with his plans and slid down to the floor at the top of the staircase, envisioning what the future would soon hold for him and the women held prison to his every whim and command.

Those women were both clueless to his schemes and evil designs on their well-being. Lady Jane still dozed, and Reba Jean went about her lazy meanderings and musings. This was the calm before the storm that they had no clue was upon them. Sid slid out of their reality and back to his realm to gather some forces in case the golden Sword was activated. That sword wouldn't get them all if he had help from the imps and minions of the underworld.

Reba Jean rose from her spot of thoughtful repose and decided to make some lunch. She had lost five ounces finally, so she needed to be careful what she ate. This whole diet business was very distracting and disconcerting. She wished she knew the secret but was sure it involved harder work than what she was already doing. Hard work seemed to be the bane of her existence these days when she did not sleep well. She did not understand why she felt so lazy and tired still. Putting away these musings, she made herself a salad. At least the housework allotted for today was basically done. She had cut a few corners, though, telling herself that scrubbing the floor on her hand and knees and removing iodine stains from the white counter was good enough.

Two books flopped off the shelves and landed on the floor; misty tendrils formed themselves into quills and began to write. It was the books that Reba Jean was using for quotes and research for the book that she was writing. Curious as to what she had thought of this time, Lady Jane walked over and watched as the words formed themselves from the thoughts.

"My friends are real. They just choose to live in books." Oh my, that was definitely interesting to ponder. Oh, here was another one about letting Jesus transform your life, as that was His business. Oh, she hoped Reba Jean would keep that in mind; this library needed transforming by Lord Rabboni.

The quills furiously scribbled more quotes that were so applicable to books being the lifeline of society and civilization. Lady Jane stopped reading and hoped that maybe Reba Jean was finally understanding the reality of this library of theirs. Or maybe she was just scrolling mindlessly on social media, and it wasn't more than just the thoughts being immortalized between the pages of a book of quotes. The misty quills paused in mid-air, waiting for the next quote to activate them.

Lady Jane watched in awe as a golden swirl from the Ancient One wrote the next words on the open page. It read, "But I know thy abode, and thy going out, and thy coming in, and thy rage against me," then an explanation by the Venerable Nobleman Tuck! Tuck was the life partner of Lady Constance and a heralder for King Abba. He was on social media talking about how King Abba knows his whereabouts, his ways (actions, words, thoughts), and his wickedness. "God help us to live like we know He knows." Lady Jane was excited to see words from the Ancient One and Nobleman Tuck get inscribed in this book. The thought of what was stated, however, grabbed her! Was Reba Jean paying attention?

Lady Jane was curious about the world outside the library. She had often wondered about it, but it had been so chaotic inside that she did not want to even look as to what was causing it from the outside. As soon as she thought about climbing up to the two windows to see out, the orchestrated hymns came to an abrupt stop. The silence was deafening and a bit disconcerting. The rain had stopped, and the ticking clock was very loud. She paused mid-step and looked around. She almost thought maybe Sid was around; it would be just like him to ruin a good mood. She glanced back up at the windows and saw sunshine streaming through. That was a good sign, wasn't it?

The quills ascended back into the mists of muse, the books softly closed, and she placed them back on their shelves in order. Now what? Soon she heard the soft clatter of fingers on the keyboard. Reba Jean must be writing her book again. Maybe some of these quotes had opened her mind to what was really going on up here in this library of theirs.

Reba Jean looked at the sunshine but heard the wind still howling. The music had turned off after hours of playing. She had found some quotes she liked, and she pondered on some of them as she typed in her novel. Were book characters all the friends she had? She then thought about that verse from this morning; God indeed did know the thoughts and intents of her heart, her ways, her comings, and goings. Did she live like He knew every minute detail of her? If He knew what was in her library, and He did, then what was she going to do about it? Her attitude of "do it another time" was not going to meet with the Lord's approval. He knew her wickedness; that's what the Scriptures had stated. *Oh Lord, my God, how wicked I have been in Thy sight; I am not worthy to be called Your daughter*, she prayed inwardly.

She felt her stomach tie in knots; she had work to do upstairs in the library, and the thought of it scared her. Pausing in mid-thought, she tossed around in her mind what to do. She really did not want to go back and deal with filth and corruption in her library. The door was locked up there; surely it was fine to leave locked for now, wasn't it? The quietness of the room and the loud ticking of the clock made her very restless. She got up to drink some water and thought about going back to mindless scrolling on social media. She had found some good quotes for her book; it wasn't completely a waste of time, she reasoned to herself.

She flounced away to spot clean a few more things in the kitchen, feeling her stomach roil even more. She needed to finish deep cleaning the library, but the thought of going up there made her nauseous. She didn't want to open the door or disturb Lady Jane. No, it would be better if she just went and laid down for a few minutes to see if the nausea passed. It was probably the lunch she ate; surely it wasn't conviction upsetting her stomach.

Lady Jane saw dust fall in clumps to the floor, but it wasn't the golden dust motes; it was old thoughts that had been hanging around and not written in any books. She wasn't sure what she should do with those wayward thoughts. They didn't seem to have a place designed to hold them. She sensed Reba Jean's unease, and she hoped that her afternoon wasn't about to erupt in destruction. Reba Jean really needed to pray more and think less, Lady Jane thought to herself. Maybe she should tell her that the next time they were together. She would probably get rebuked for her cheekiness. The Overseer would be coming for an inspection any day now. What would He find? Was this a place suitable for Lord Rabboni to walk through? Lady Jane knew what He would say if He opened the door to that upper room. His upper rooms were holy places of fellowship and service, not slave markets of sin.

Reba Jean almost shivered; she wasn't cold—she just didn't feel right. Sometimes, she wondered if she played the hymns because, like King Saul of old, they seem to keep out the evil spirits. Usually, the quiet did not bother her; in fact, she welcomed it. Today, however, it felt just as cloudy as the clouds outside. She paused, trying to justify in her mind that she was fine, the doors upstairs were locked, and she didn't need to disturb any dusty tomes or murky corners.

She decided it was time to go back to scrolling through social media posts. That would take her mind off of any sort of dirty work. In the middle of her scrolling, this verse leaped off the screen at her. 1 Peter 3:12 "For the eyes of the Lord are over the righteous, and his ears open unto their prayers: but the face of the Lord is against them that do evil." Her stomach dropped; which was she, righteous or evil if she left that room intact upstairs?

Lady Jane saw the Ancient One start flipping its pages. Curiosity led her to see what the golden words highlighted. Oh! This was a strong warning from the Ancient One; the Overseer must be down in the living room already.

Chapter 7

Reba Jean felt the conviction of the Holy Spirit at the reading of these words from Scripture. He often used social media posts to get her attention, but she needed to deal with the besetting sins and weights that dragged down her spiritual walk. She curled up in her prayer spot and let the Holy Spirit deal with her thought life. All those past issues had been put under His blood, except that room of forbidden lust and debauchery. Oh, it wasn't in active use, but it had not been fully taken care of once and for all. As she spent time in prayer, she realized that she had been given the power to overcome the wiles of the devil. If sin was getting into her life, she was allowing it. Sitting there thinking about Sid, she asked the Holy Spirit to show her what to do about him.

He pointed her to the Scriptures about how to deal with the devil and his treacherous ways. Her eyes widened as she realized that Sid was a representation of Satan and his minions. He was wandering around almost freely in her library. Wait, her library? What was her library actually? Reba Jean sat thunderstruck as the realization of what the library truly was came to light. She dropped to her knees and begged God to help her with the task ahead.

Lady Jane sensed that something was definitely changing. The air seemed charged with expectation; the Ancient One was flipping through its pages, and the books were trembling on their shelves. The Overseer was coming, and things were going to be changed around this old library. Lady Jane waited a few minutes; then curiosity got the best of her. She pulled over a chair and some shelves and made a makeshift ladder to look out the windows overhead. She looked down to see Reba Jean curled up on the floor of the living room. Was she ok? Oh, she was sobbing and praying. This was a good thing, wasn't it? Lady Jane looked around at Reba Jean's world; it was so strangely different than the library and yet felt familiar all the same. She felt a sense of restlessness come over her and swayed on her precarious ladder. If she wasn't careful, she would end up smashing herself onto the library floor. She had seen the story of Humpty Dumpty in a childhood book before; she did not want to end up like that character. Getting back down gingerly, she wondered what would happen next. Reba Jean and the Overseer were long overdue for a visit. Would Sid appear? What sort of battle would erupt? Lady Jane quivered in excited anticipation; what if the King Himself was coming?

She wandered back over to the Ancient One and began reading about sanctifying the Lord God in your hearts, have a good conscience... She stopped, a good conscience... that meant HER! She was Reba Jean's conscience created by the King to listen to the Overseer. Another page flipped, and she read, "And when the chief Shepherd shall appear, ye shall receive a crown of glory that fadeth not away." And, "Humble yourselves therefore under the mighty hand of God..."

Lady Jane's eyes filled with tears; the King was coming soon. Would she be found faithful?

The library came to a standstill as both Reba Jean and Lady Jane communed respectively with the Almighty. Sid, passing by, felt a shock go through him as he touched the door to the library. His finger traced the symbol he had left on it, but it seemed to be fading. Something was going on. He would need to gather his forces; it was nearly time to take full control of this library and the whimpering women inside.

Sid went back to his underworld realm and started recruiting his army of evil minions. That Sword and the Ancient One would be overwhelmed by the evil that he would pour out in his wrath. He would be the captain of the horde; oh, the thought pleased him to no end. He craved control and power of any sort but especially over mindless human creatures.

Reba Jean blew her nose, wiped her tears, and went to get a cup of coffee. She felt cleaner, but her stomach still felt tied in knots. A faint thought about a swept house and evil coming back in seven times stronger played in the fringe of her consciousness. She did not pay as much attention to it as she should have, as she would learn later. Bolstered with the courage to take care of business in the library, she still procrastinated, believing that the locked door was deterrent enough.

Lady Jane waited in anticipation expecting the door to swing open any second. Instead, nothing happened. Lady Jane crossed her arms and slumped down in a defiant heap of pity. Reba Jean sure could prolong the agony, now couldn't she?

Reba Jean fixed herself some coffee and a snack and tried to remind herself of the things she would soon need to get busy with—supper, the funeral visitation, pulling dinner rolls out to rise for the funeral dinner, and checking the mail. Just little things, but she played them over and over like a broken record so that she would not forget to do them. She could obsess over nothing, thus filling her mind with numbness. She still needed to learn that actual obedience was immediate, not in some distant future. The Lord would continue to convict and deal with her the next few days over her slothfulness.

She did not normally want to write on Sundays; this was a day set aside to worship and honor her Lord Jesus. However, over the weekend, He had really been convicting her of some of the things she had been doing (or had not been doing). She had even looked up the definition of guilt versus conviction. When the Creator of the universe convicts you of something, it is the first step towards change. She had not let that change happen; thus, she felt guilty but hadn't followed through with what needed to be done. She realized that some, if not all, of what she was thinking was completely affecting the library. This weekend she had allowed things to go through her mind that were vile and irreprehensible. She had been on a journey to let Jesus transform her mind over the last few years. As much progress as had been made, it took just a word or television show or social media post to trigger her mind into something carnal or worse.

This book had started out to be a way to air her family secrets and thus supposedly bring closure to her past. Instead, the Holy Spirit had convicted her of putting these things under the blood, letting go of the past, and renewing her mind. She had to do this by taking every thought captive. Too many times, the thoughts held her captive instead. She was their prisoner, and they were her masters, enslaving her to the corrupt mindset. Lady Jane was not the one who should be in charge of her mental library. With the help of the Holy Spirit, she could have a transformed mind. It was time to stop being so wishy-washy about it.

Yes, it was time to truly clean the library from top to bottom!

Lady Jane hadn't seen Reba Jean for days now. She had been so excited when she thought the Overseer was coming to their library. She knew He monitored everything, and she had felt His presence often, but He did seem to stay in the living room more often than in the upstairs library. She hoped that

Reba Jean was getting a better idea about what the library was and its true purpose. She was scared about this book being written; she had had too many traumatizing experiences here in the library with books being written.

Looking around, she felt the atmosphere was calm, and a sense of peace permeated the main floor. She could hear gaming sounds from Sir Theo's library. When would Reba Jean return? What was keeping her from cleaning the library and making it ready for King Abba and Lord Rabboni? A touch of panic welled up in Lady Jane's chest when she thought of the Royal Family coming to this library.

Clasping her hands together under her chin, she tried to breathe evenly and slowly. She had no desire to attract Sid's attention; he sure did thrive on drama and fear. She needed to communicate somehow to Reba Jean; this whole book business needed to be wrapped up in a way that was pleasing to the King. Material that she had intended to use to vindicate her and vilify others was not what was actually happening.

"…taking every thought captive…" she needed to stop letting her thoughts run amok and make them obedient to Christ. With this intention, she decided to run upstairs to the library to visit Lady Jane. Together, they would need to finish this monumental task of transforming and renewing her mind. She knew she had to have the Holy Spirit help her. He had already told her what to take care of, so she had best do it!

Reba Jean opened the door to the library; the chime made a squawk that unnerved her for a minute. Surveying the atrium and main floor, she wondered why it felt so unnaturally calm. It felt more like a calm before a storm, waiting for the next shoe to drop. She jumped as a shoe dropped in front of her from a storm cloud above. Oh my! Her thoughts came to life as soon as she thought them.

She walked through the aisles, trying to be very careful what she thought about. She noticed the blue butterflies flittering around, and that brought a smile to her face. A rainbow arced across a wooden beam and filtered into beautiful hued dust motes across the walkway. She did not call out or try to make a sound; she just checked the aisles to ensure that they were in order. She knew she would eventually discover Lady Jane's location.

Lady Jane heard a horrible squawk, and thinking it was a vulture coming to get her, she slid under the settee to hide. Not hearing anything further, she peeked out and then withdrew quickly, just avoiding bumping her head on the underside of the cushion. Footsteps were softly approaching, and she felt fear. Two feet stood in front of her settee and stood there. She looked at them; no, they did not appear to be Sid's or any of the Royal Family's. Were they Reba Jean's? Before she could decide, there was a soft sound of clothing crumpling into a heap on the floor; two beautiful blue eyes peered into hers. It was Reba Jean, and she had found Lady Jane hiding. Why indeed was Lady Jane hiding? Reba Jean looked around, trying not to feel alarmed; she did not want any interruptions of tendrils and books flying around.

"Lady Jane, my dear?" whispered Reba Jean softly, "Are you well? Please tell me you are just playing hide and seek with me?"

"I am so glad it's you. I was afraid it was Sid or even the King, and we are not ready for either to be here!" Lady Jane timidly replied.

Reba Jean helped Lady Jane slide out unhurt from her hiding place under the settee. They both remained on the floor and stared at each other. How much longer they had together remained to be seen. If Reba Jean took control of the library as she should, what would Lady Jane do?

Tilting her head in concentration, Reba Jean tried to mentally communicate with Lady Jane without saying a word. Was mental telepathy possible between the two of them? She thought of peaceful things, reassuring words of comfort, and the blue butterflies flitted over their heads, skipping over rainbow-hued dust motes.

Lulled by the stilled beauty, the storm cloud had dissipated into the mists of muse; the two women sat quietly together. They were not lost in thought, more so just enjoying their camaraderie in the peace on this Lord's Day.

A beautiful strand of golden words from the Ancient One formed a circle around them. It read, "Be still and know that I am God." They both breathed in the presence of the Holy One Who had joined their gathering. "Where two or three are gathered together in my name, there am I in the midst" was almost audible as it too circled its golden ring around them, making them feel safe and secure.

Reba Jean's husband came looking for her right in the middle of her moment of peace. She felt the distraction and even wondered if Sid had sent him. She knew this was dangerous; even the thought of Sid could conjure him up, or so it seemed. She huffed inwardly to herself and could not seem to recapture the moment of peace. Her stomach was tied in knots, and her head started hurting again. It seemed as if the work on the library and her good intentions were going to have to wait another day. She knew tomorrow had a full schedule, but she also knew she needed more time in prayer in order to tackle this monumental task.

She leaned in towards Lady Jane, silently gave her a reassuring hug, and then exited the library. She hoped Lady Jane understood, maybe even better than she herself did. So much work to do, and it never seemed like it got anywhere. Did

Lady Jane feel this way too? She always had books to supervise, organize, catalog, and all sorts of things flowing through the library all the time. People, places, plans, all of these had to be filtered and analyzed and processed accordingly. Reba Jean felt a bit intimidated by all the stuff that surged through her library, seemingly uncontrolled. She could definitely make the processing easier and simpler; she just had to take control of what went through her library.

As usual, any time that Reba Jean felt overwhelmed, she would find some menial household task to do. That way, she felt like she was getting something done, even if it wasn't what was the more important thing that needed her attention.

What would happen when the book was off to the publisher? It had been such a wondrous companion in her mind these last few weeks. Was there another book that the Lord wanted her to write? She reflected on the job offer she had received this past week, from a previous employer that she had worked for many years ago. She pondered some other ministry outreaches, wondering if she was supposed to get involved with those again as well. She did not believe she was, as of yet. That in itself was a bit puzzling to her. She stared off into space, saved her place in her manuscript, and wandered off, pondering what the Lord wanted her to do for Him more than she was already.

Reba Jean was busy with regular life for the next few days; she hadn't really been to the library to truly see what was going on in there. If anything, she stayed away from it for various reasons. Sunday night, the preacher had really preached right down her row, as they say. She took notes because she knew the Lord was telling her she needed to fix her thought life. These were not new verses that he referenced, but she definitely knew they were the exact ones that God wanted her to hear. He also expected her to obey, not just hear them. She was great at procrastination, though. Monday was her lecture time with the beginner librarians, and she had gone to see a special widow friend that she had neglected to visit for too many long months. She wondered why it seemed she was just as busy now as she was when she was working. People still wore her out; even if the causes and the acts of those issues were under the blood of Jesus, the aftermath still had to be dealt with properly. Too many times, she reacted instead of being proactive about preventing the thoughts from running a marathon in her head. She knew she needed to stop watching television, especially vivid crime shows, but it seemed to be a habit she had yet to break for long.

Reba Jean looked at her notes from Sunday night, trying to recapture the thoughts she had. Her new prayer closet was a total distraction; she knew that even if it was comfortable, it wasn't a true prayer closet, and she would need to find another that wasn't full of extra distractions. So her prayer life seemed minimal; she couldn't seem to focus on the sermon notes. She just felt so distracted about everything. Her husband told her that he was depressed, and her widow friend said she was depressed too. Her daughter-in-law had asked for prayer because she was overburdened by all the thoughts in her mind. Reba Jean needed something to change desperately before she ended up depressed as well. She had grown up in an era where depression was taboo for Christians. Moreover, sickness was seen and labeled as a result of sin, so any time you were sick, you were in obvious rebellion. The Bible says rebellion is as the sin of witchcraft, so it was enough to make you even question your salvation. Everything was about appearances, so you needed to appear to be fine. Anything actually wrong was to be hidden away and not even discussed.

Reba Jean realized this is why it had taken her a long time to process all the various evil things that had happened to her or her family members because the sin was not dealt with properly, and it was not something to be discussed, analyzed, or processed in a healthy spiritual manner. Mental health was a huge issue being brought to light now that she was older, and she was beginning to realize that it seemed nearly everyone had some sort of mental health issue. The way to analyze, process, and deal with mental health was to discover its source. If you do not know what is causing it, how can you properly help the person?

Romans 8:5-6 from her sermon notes stated, "For they that are after the flesh do mind the things of the flesh; but they that are after the Spirit the things of the Spirit. For to be carnally minded is death; but to be spiritually minded is life and peace." She then flipped over to Romans 13:14, "But put ye on the Lord Jesus Christ, and make not provision for the flesh, to fulfil the lusts thereof."

She sat and pondered these two verses from Scripture. Part of her mental problem was based on her fleshly wants, and she was not minding the things of the Spirit. She knew this was probably the cause of so many people's mental problems. How do you deal with this? Well, her preacher had stated it was by knowing that we have victory through the Lord Jesus Christ over problems, even the mental ones.

Reba Jean paused in her review of the sermon. Again, the Lord was telling her to clean up her mind and to get the dirt out of it. Why did she take so long to be obedient? Was she prolonging mental health issues that could be fixed? The Lord said He had victory for her to overcome, to be more than a conqueror through Him. Maybe, she didn't want victory? Maybe, she was so used to being a victim that she felt justified in her wounds or in dredging up vile acts in her mind.

She really needed to fix her issues, or she would never be able to help her husband, her friend, her daughter-in-law, or whoever else might come her way needing hope, help, healing, and mental health that can be found in the Word of God.

Chapter 8

Sid saw that he needed to add a few more soldiers to his army before he reclaimed the library for himself. He had already enlisted Mayhem and Chaos. He liked to use those to create such a ruckus that defeat was usually quick and long-lasting. He recruited Distraction and Depression to help them keep it dark and moody and busy during the siege. Looking around, he finally asked who else wanted to go wreak havoc with him for the dark lord of the underworld.

The assault commenced; the door to the upstairs secret room was unlocked with the copy of the iron key he had made from Reba Jean's carelessness. The lurid lights and noises permeated the library. He rushed down to the Ancient One and the Golden Sword and threw a dark mantle of laziness over them. He directed the imps to have fun with the fountain of living water. They spit in it and dribbled black ooze all around it, then pulled down the misty tendrils and created a wall of thorns to encase it. Running around, they spied Lady Jane hiding yet again under the settee. Pulling her out by her ankles, cackling at her screams, they presented her to Mr. Insidious for his pleasure.

Mr. Insidious, looking very powerful and menacing, pulled her to his side, declared that she belonged to him, and shackled her to his bony wrist. Waving his sharp dagger around, he carved out a room from one of the walled-in alcoves. There he placed huge tv screens that played all sorts of movies and tv shows from Reba Jean's own selections. Mayhem and Chaos ran around knocking over books, tearing out pages, and leaving black ooze everywhere they went. The dust motes were held at bay by dark storm clouds cast by Depression, who had brought Discouragement along with him.

They found the archway to Sir Theo's library and destroyed one of his hard drives, stirred up his golden bees into a swarm of angry, pain-filled creatures that could only buzz in protest. Sid tried to open the Crimson Vault but couldn't, so he pulled around bookshelves and chests to block it from being opened by anyone else. Summoning Apathy from the underworld, he directed him to take Distraction and start to work on the walls of the library.

Noticing the two beautiful windows near the ceiling, he drew out a cloak of sleep and threw it up there to cover them. Now it was time to change the sound system; he re-wired it to play ungodly music and criticisms and doubt-filled words into the library. This place was starting to look more like it used to before that stupid Lady Jane had been placed in charge. He glanced at her as she cowered and whimpered next to him. His claw-like finger stroked her face and left an open wound, which filled with black ooze and putrification.

Feeling satisfied and pleased with his reclamation of the library, he twirled the long ladle, forming and shaping it into a scepter. He then waved it a few more times, conjuring up a throne to sit on in the middle of the library. Dragging Lady Jane along with him, he sat regally on his throne and surveyed his newly renovated domain.

Lady Jane felt powerless and completely at the mercy of Mr. Insidious. She had ceased to stop her outward screams for mercy and help. Inwardly though, she felt like she was banging her head on a brick wall. The black ooze in her wound made her ache all over, and her skin crawled and itched. She just wanted to die; that surely was better than all of this mayhem and chaos. She wanted to hear the songs of Lord Rabboni, not the filth playing through the sound system. She was scared of the swarm of angry bees from Sir Theo's library coming to sting and torment her.

The library looked so vastly different than it had in years. She had barely kept it clean and organized; she understood this was what she had been fighting against for the last few years. Today, yes, this was the day she was defeated; it was pointless to even try to follow the Overseer's requests. It was futile to even try to please Lord Rabboni. She didn't think King Abba loved her anymore, surely not with how everything was now. She was a slave of Mr. Insidious, and she might as well just give in and let him do whatever he was going to do. She hoped that Reba Jean would kill herself and put them both out of their misery.

The heaviness of depression and sleep surrounded Lady Jane, and she eventually closed her eyes and whimpered off to sleep. When Reba Jean slept, Lady Jane had a vastly different task; she had to watch the dreams and wake Reba Jean when they would get to be too much or too evil. Lady Jane rarely slept except when she was under anesthesia. Now, she was in her own nightmare world of sleep. It was over; she had failed King Abba. She wasn't strong enough to overcome all of this ungodliness.

Reba Jean sat in her chair and stared off into space. The music was playing, and her Bible was open, but she just seemed a million miles away. She was getting distracted yet again, might as well just give in to it. She didn't think she was really ADHD or even ADD, but it sure seemed like it at times. She felt sleepy again and thought of taking a nap, but her mind was going in all sorts of directions, and she did not think she could rest. The music was meant to be soothing and draw her closer to the Lord, but it wasn't having the effect it usually did. The idea of going to the library just seemed too daunting. She knew it needed to be taken care of, but as in the previous days, she just put it off for another time. Lady Jane was capable of organizing and cleaning; she would just leave her alone and let her do her job. Who needed Reba Jean up there anyway; she probably caused more chaos when she was up there than when she stayed away.

Reba Jean wandered off to snack on a banana and mumble about diets and weight loss.

Sleepiness overcame Reba Jean even stronger; she felt like the music was lulling her to sleep. Maybe that was a good thing. What trouble would it cause if she just took a nap; it was her time to do what she wanted, wasn't it?

Dozing off into a daydream, Reba Jean stopped searching the Scriptures or even doing anything physical, spiritual, or mental.

The banana had left a bad taste in her mouth; she grumbled some more and flopped down on the couch with her cup of water. Ugh, what a nasty taste…

She closed her eyes in disgust and felt restless in spite of the overpowering fatigue. The restlessness won out over the perpetual desire to sleep. She answered some messages she saw on her phone, unloaded the dishwasher, and started letting the hymns of Zion permeate her consciousness. Verses started popping up, and she felt a sense of determination overtake her.

Stepping up to the door to the library, she tried to open it. It felt like it was heavy and blocked. She couldn't seem to budge it. She couldn't believe that she couldn't access her own library. The doorknob turned, so it wasn't locked; it just seemed inaccessible. She put her ear up to the door to see if she could hear anything. The noise was muted but unmistakable; she realized knocking was probably pointless. It sounded like a riot at a rock concert in there, and that was from outside the door. She was appalled as to what she would find inside. She looked around and spotted something she could use for leverage; she managed to pry the door open enough to slip inside. That was a tight fit, and her body felt bruised from squeezing through the narrow opening. She did not want an open mind, but a steel trap was not a good idea either. She looked around and was not even sure what she was seeing. It was so dark and overcast inside, creepy crawly things skittered around, and she felt like she had entered a beehive. She saw two glowing eyes fastened on her, and she felt drawn to them in spite of a feeling of dread and panic welling up in her. It seemed almost against her will and yet not; she approached the glowing eyes that lured her closer. She saw Sid sitting on a throne at the other end of the atrium. Shackled to his arm was Lady Jane in some sort of stupor. She had an oozing wound on her face, and she looked deathly pale.

Reba Jean's eyes widened, and she was about to speak out in alarm and consternation. Before, she could even voice her outrage, Sid stood up, slid his other arm around her and drew her down the corridor. He stopped outside the archway to Sir Theo's library and cackled at her expression. Then he proceeded to silently and triumphantly give her a tour of HIS library. She shrunk back in disgust from the room of pornography that was unlocked again. He pulled her in and forced her to look around. Then he dragged her to the multimedia room he had created. She saw all the tv shows and movies that she had ever watched, the videos, and social media posts from over the years all playing on screens from floor to ceiling. He waved his scepter, and the room expanded upwards into the higher levels of the library until they disappeared except for their glow of light into the very rafters of the library.

Everything was dark, depressing, loud, and chaotic; she couldn't even think. The music of Zion could not be heard in here, and she had no idea where the Crimson Door was now or the Ancient One and the Golden Sword. In desperation, she looked around for the Fountain of Living Water and saw imps playing around it, casting vile-looking things into it, trying to pollute it.

Feeling something itchy, she looked down to see a creature scratching her back and arms. He wrapped his hairy paws around her and nestled close to her chest like a cat. Sid laughed and said, "Awe, looks like you have found a pet to keep you company. What will you name it?" Although it made her itch, she did have a soft heart for anything that seemed to like her or pay attention to her. She looked at Sid, and he suggested a nickname of Conte'. She did not know yet that its real name was Discontent.

Reba Jean just did not know what to think of this complete and utter transformation of the library. She had an idea that it could be like this or that it had been in the past. She had, however, thought that the little changes she had made through the years were enough. Maybe it was futile to change. Sid was just too powerful, and who was she to constantly fight the inevitable? She did not seem to really notice when Sid linked his claw-like fingers with hers creating a bond with her.

They all walked back to his throne room, and he sat down to weave a tale of enticement and allurement of all that he could offer them and what a life they could all have together. His version of "happily ever after" was vastly different than what Reba Jean had envisioned, but after all, she had been duped by the King, or so Sid said. Reba Jean and Lady Jane both fell into a stupor of laziness and apathy as Sid droned on about all his accomplishments.

Soft, sweet words to a hymn filtered into Reba Jean's subconsciousness—*Nearer my God to Thee*. Her eyes widened; she again felt repulsed by the closeness of Sid. Before either of them realized it, she tore herself from his grasp, ran for the door, and slammed it shut behind her. What on earth was she going to do? *Nearer my God to Thee, nearer to Thee...* it kept drawing her.

She ran to the living room, collapsed on her knees, and begged God to help her. She truly did want to get close to Him. She had a mess in her mental library, and only He could clean it out for her. She prayed earnestly for help. She needed that

94

transformed mind; she needed victory. Who was Sid, and why was he there?

The Holy Spirit brought to mind the verses that she had labeled LSD. James 1:13-15 "Let no man say when he is tempted, I am tempted of God: for God cannot be tempted with evil, neither tempteth he any man: But every man is tempted, when he is drawn away of his own Lust, and enticed. Then when lust hath conceived, it bringeth forth Sin: and sin, when it is finished, bringeth forth Death." Lust, Sin, Death—that's what was going on in her library right now! Why was this happening? She was saved, she was serving the Lord, she read her Bible every day, she prayed; why was she having this takeover in her library?

In agony, she cried out to God to show her the truth. He reminded her of the message that He had been trying to show her for weeks now. Sid was Mr. Insidious; just calling him Sid made him too familiar. She had gotten familiar with Sinister Sid. Sin lures us in, our flesh gets comfortable, and then we get apathetic and lazy. *Do not let sin reign in our mortal bodies* came rushing into her mind. Sin and Sid were connected, and in order for her to have a transformed mind, she needed to not just clean it but replace all the old with all the new. When we get too familiar with sin, it becomes flammable, and we become fruitless, her preacher had stated.

Looking some more at James 1, she saw the verse about a double-minded man being unstable in all his ways. Boy, did that also apply to her. Further on down the chapter, she read that she needed to be a doer of the Word, not just a hearer only. She had not been completely obedient; she had only half cleaned her library. Remembering the song that had awakened her from her sin-filled stupor, she flipped over to James 4:7-8 and read, "Submit yourselves therefore to God. Resist the devil, and he will flee from you. Draw nigh to God, and he will draw nigh to you. Cleanse your hands, ye sinners; and purify your hearts, ye double minded."

Her breath caught, her hands fluttered and itched, and her heart raced. She had the tools right here to deal with Mr. Insidious and her messed-up mental library. She knew her library was her mind, and what went into it was stored there forever. She might have thought of it as a sponge, but everything that went into her porous gray matter was written and stored. Some of it never appeared again, but too many times, whatever she put in there came out in her actions, her words, and even in her reactions.

Let this mind be in you, which was also in Christ Jesus... ran through her spirit. I can have the mind of Christ, the Bible says so, but I have to be a doer of the Word, not just a hearer only. It was time to truly clean the library. To resist the devil embodied in Mr. Insidious, take control of what was supposed to be in her mind, to remove the Lust, Sin, and Death (LSD) that was trying to control her. Lady Jane might be her conscience, but she had the Holy Spirit, and He was Truth, and in Him was no error. Her conscience wasn't to be in control; the Holy Spirit was!

She would need to put on the armor of God, protect herself, and keep the familiar sin from getting too familiar or too close. She had the victory through the Lord Jesus Christ to overcome this; He would fight for her. She needed peace of mind, and Mr. Insidious was no longer going to be able to just stroll in whenever he pleased.

Reba Jean felt invigorated, but she knew once she got back into the library, it might be a different story. She would have the Ancient One, the Golden Sword, her armor, the shield of faith, but she needed courage. She was afraid she would give up if the fight got too long or hard. She noticed the sunshine seemed to get increasingly brighter through the window. She looked at it and then saw dark storm clouds gathering. The sun always seemed brighter when clouds were darkened behind it. She had to face the storm clouds; this library of secrets needed to be a library of celestial sanctuary. Her need to be vindicated for all the evil that had affected her throughout her life was rooted in pride. She did not need to be the victim but the victor; she had stated this before, but now she used it to encourage herself for the battle ahead.

Inhaling, she stopped for a minute to listen to the hymn that was now playing on the sound system. She would need to fix that mental sound system again so that the hymns could be heard once again, not ungodly music. "When I survey the Wondrous Cross" streamed through the house; what a beautiful reminder about what the Lord had done for her. He wanted to bury her past and her sins to be remembered no more. She had to stop digging them up and putting them on display in her mind.

Chapter 9

Reba Jean pondered something stated by a well-known public figure about analyzing the root of things, especially behaviors. A lot of mental and emotional digging around, searching for the source, and hopefully, a subsequent solution was something that dogged her daily. Usually, the roots were found to be from a source of flesh, sin, and pride. Not very good sources to be grounded and established to achieve peace.

Looking through some more memes, it was evident that some of these needed to be on the walls of her library. For example, "She's never where she is; she's only inside her head." She did NOT want to be inside her head right now, not until it was purified.

Another meme stated

"Why I'm 'Quiet':
- I already dealt with people today
- I'm reading
- The world in my head is better
- I don't see the point of small talk
- I don't like that many people

She looked at this meme, she knew this described her perfectly, yet she also knew that she could do better at "peopling."

It was time; she did not feel ready, but it was necessary. Putting on her armor, clasping her shield of faith tightly, she knelt in prayer, asking the Lord God of Heaven to fight for her. Tramping up the stairs resolutely, she yanked open the door, refusing to let it resist her. She stomped in and went straight to work. Taking her own copy of the Golden Sword that she usually kept in the living room, she brandished it high and sure. She began clearing the entrance around the Crimson Vault first. It was still locked, thankfully.

Mr. Insidious felt some resistance enter the library. He sensed that things were not the same in his realm at the moment. He summoned his minions and army and ordered them to battle stations! This was going to be a battle, but he would win—he always did. He played the long game all the time; this was just a little skirmish like the others. This time he would show her who was boss. She would bow before him and make HIM king like he used to be.

He rose to what looked like an enormous height, puffed out his chest, and dragged Lady Jane along beside him as he went to meet his foe. Mr. Insidious saw Reba Jean in her suit of armor, brandishing another Golden Sword that looked just as sharp as the one he had hidden away. He knew better than to show fear, though, so he turned to mocking her and criticizing her instead. He railed against her show of strength and gave the command to his minions to fire away!

Reba Jean saw Mr. Insidious for the bully that he was as the fiery darts began to descend upon her from all directions. She raised her shield and met them head-on but with protection. She swung her sword towards the fountain of living water. It connected with the silver that was under the ooze, and the chime that rang out sounded like a war cry of an archangel. The ooze and the creatures fled from the fountain as if a holy fire had scorched them painfully.

The Golden Sword of truth led her to find the Ancient One that was buried under a heap of darkness and soot. She cleared all of that away and opened It up. A golden ray of words sprang out and empowered the sword leaning at its base. The golden rays shot upward, and like fireworks on the Fourth of July, the clouds of discontentment and the evil discord that was being sewn into the very fabric of the library were cut away. The dust motes were embodied again with the Word of God, and it was starting to look more celestial inside the living library.

Mr. Insidious growled ferociously like a wounded beast and reached out to pluck a book out of thin air. He handed it to Reba Jean; its title read, "Your OUGHT TO BIOGRAPHY." He laughed as she let it drop to the floor.

He fully expected her to turn tail and run out of the library like she had done all the other times. Reba Jean looked at the title of her own book about her life. All the things she should have done were there written down incriminating her. She felt the fiery darts hit her shield, but as her hand faltered in defeat, she caught a glimpse of something out of the side of her eye. Lady Jane was still shackled to the demon!

Reba Jean felt a burst of strength empower her; she needed to save Lady Jane and her library. She was a child of the King, a soldier of the cross; she was NOT doing this in her own strength. With renewed vigor, she swung the book of good intentions with the tip of her Sword, and it landed on the shelf, closed and locked again.

Making her way with Sword and Shield in hand, she began praying and calling out to God to clean this mess. She asked forgiveness for the pornographic material, and that room was soon cleared out. She then proceeded to the multimedia room that Sid had engineered to reflect her bad habit. She stuck the Golden Sword into the power outlet, and it fritzed out the whole network. With sparks shooting and the sound warbling to an end, the room went quiet. Finally, she touched the wires, and golden dust motes descended to rework the wiring to allow the songs of Zion to be played again over the sound system inside these porous walls.

Reba Jean looked around; it was still a cluttered, nasty, oozy mess in there; she had only just tackled the largest obstacles. Mr. Insidious was still there, and Lady Jane was still shackled. She walked over to the Ancient One to find direction in her next task. She read its words of hope, help, and healing and again swung the Golden Sword in a huge, down-sweeping arc. Lady Jane was freed from her shackles!

Lady Jane aroused from her stupor, rubbed her wrist where she had been bound, and looked around to see what was happening. The sight was a vision to behold! She knew Reba Jean had an active imagination, but this was real! She rubbed the wound on her cheek and felt a tingle. She looked up to see a golden strand dip into the fountain of living water and then touch her wound. The wound healed, the black ooze shrieked as it was pulled from the spot, and the wound then became a closed scar. Lady Jane might always carry the scar, but it never had to be an infected wound ever again.

Mr. Insidious howled; this fight was NOT over. He still had Sir Theo's library, and the library still had Mayhem and Chaos. The windows were still covered; he hadn't lost this fight yet! He rallied his forces again, breathing out threats and evil suggestions, berating her for thinking that she was holier than he was. He had been to Heaven itself, she hadn't; who did she think she was?

Reba Jean faltered at the verbal and mental castrations of the evil one. Then she heard the beautiful strains of the song playing on the sound system. It was telling her not to be discouraged but to take it to the Lord in prayer. She dropped to her knees, praying aloud as she swung the Golden Sword. She heard an unholy shriek, and she watched the imp named Discouragement fade out into the nether world. She kept praying and swinging the Sword of the Word of God, and she watched other minions flee as she resisted their fiery darts. That little evil cat-like creature came up next, and she saw its collar said "Conte." She splashed some water from the fountain on it. It hissed and howled, and she saw it was of the breed of Discontentment. She splashed more living water on it, and it leaped away and disappeared with a loud hiss.

Mr. Insidious looked around to see how the battle was going; he had his scepter and his ungodly dagger swatting away dust motes and ducking blows from the Golden Swords. It just wasn't over until he said it was. Lady Jane might be free of his shackles at the moment, but he could reopen that scar and ensnare her again. Her mind wasn't all that stable; it was still pretty wishy-washy, he could tell as she stood there uncertainly.

Reba Jean paused to catch her breath; she was breathing heavily, and the battle was tiring her out. There was still so much left to do; this place did indeed look like a war zone. Looking around, she needed to see what else needed to be done. See… *it's still hard to see in here,* she thought to herself. She looked up at the windows; they were still heavily cloaked in sleep and apathy. While the rest of the library was being cleared of the passivity and laziness that had overshadowed it, the windows were still so darkened that they looked like they had drapes pulled over them.

Reba Jean did not know how to reach up that high unless she was going to pull over bookshelves. She knew that was too precarious to manage while also doing battle up there without a strong support. Well, if like she had read this morning that God could open the windows of heaven if she just believed, then He could open these windows in the library. She closed her eyes and asked the Lord to remove the darkness in front of her eyes. She raised her hands in prayer and praise and waited in pure belief.

All at once, the sunshine poured in through the two beautiful windows, and a lovely azure glow permeated the upper chambers. Lady Jane raised her hands in worship and praise with Reba Jean. They closed their eyes and worshipped Lord Rabboni and King Abba. As their prayers and praises wafted toward Heaven, a lovely, strong Presence stepped into the library. The Overseer was here!!!!

"Holy, Holy, Holy, Lord God Almighty" began to play through the sound system.

Reba Jean and Lady Jane bowed in humble worship.

The Overseer assured them, strengthened them, and comforted them as they renewed their strength to finish the battle. He had never been far, but they had grieved and quenched Him. Now, He was able to do what He had been assigned to do: Convict, Convince, and Comfort these children of the King.

Mr. Insidious, seeing the Overseer was here, started grabbing whatever books he could; he needed ammunition to present his case as to why this was HIS library. He rummaged through locked chests with his copied key. Reba Jean saw his key and realized that not only had she become familiar with sin, but she had allowed it to have a key to her thoughts and mind! It was now easy to see why Mayhem and Chaos had such free rein in here! She had not been careful and had not guarded her thoughts from the evil one.

The Overseer proclaimed, "In the Name of King Abba, and Lord Rabboni, this library is now and always will be under the authority of the royal Lord of Heaven." Mr. Insidious huffed inwardly, but outwardly he started stacking up the books that had not been put in the Crimson Vault. He even had made copies of the ones that had been placed there.

He began listing all the deeds and thoughts that Reba Jean had since she was three years old. Such vile and profane thoughts, she did not deserve the protection of King Abba. She was a vile wicked creature, and vile wicked people needed justice, not mercy. Is that not what the Ancient One stated? Mr. Insidious pawed through paperwork and charts, displaying every sin or thought of sin that Reba Jean had done and Lady Jane had let slide.

Reba Jean felt nauseous, and a knot formed in the pit of her stomach as Mr. Insidious presented his well-orchestrated case against her. He was right; she did deserve hell for what she had done or thought… except for one thing.

She had confessed her sin, asked for forgiveness, and IT WAS UNDER THE BLOOD!

The Overseer looked at Mr. Insidious and then at Lady Jane and Reba Jean.

"Mr. Insidious, you are hereby banished to the nether world; be thou gone from this library! All I see is covered by the blood of Lord Rabboni, Who died for this child of King Abba. You no longer have authority; get thee hence!"

With a flashbang of smoke and sulfur, Mr. Insidious was banished to the nether realm where he belonged. Lady Jane fell into a heap before the Overseer and sobbed. Reba Jean bowed in thankful worship with tears pouring down her cheeks. Such mercy, goodness, and grace had been extended in spite of her unworthiness; she was overcome and overwhelmed. Light streamed through the windows, the songs of Zion played on the sound system, and the dust motes danced in praise to their Lord Rabboni.

The Overseer moved over to the Ancient One and flipped its pages to 1 Timothy 1:17, "Now unto the King eternal, immortal, invisible, the only wise God, be honour and glory for ever and ever. Amen."

Reba Jean arose and went over to the Ancient One and lightly caressed its pages, looking for the verse that was flowing through her thoughts right then.

2 Timothy 1:7 "For God hath not given us the spirit of fear; but of power, and of love, and of a sound mind." She knelt down and thanked the Lord for His victory over this

battle. She was aware that this was just a major battle; she was still fighting a war until she was called Home for her reward.

"Lady Jane, my dear, the Overseer has come; together with His help, we will continue to fight and be on guard to protect this library." Reba Jean assured her that the library was under rightful ownership and that she herself would exert more control over what came into the library from every entrance.

Lady Jane was weak with relief; the Overseer had not banished her, Mr. Insidious was really gone for good, and Reba Jean truly understood that it was up to her, not Lady Jane, to control what came into the library. She knew that from now on, she should have a supporting role, not a supervisory role. That is if Reba Jean stayed strong in the Lord and in the power of His might.

The Overseer changed all the locks on all the chests and gave them a new key, one that was programmed to be used only by the owner. He then went to Sir Theo's library and walked through there, assessing the damage. He turned to the ladies and instructed them to pray for Sir Theo right then and to continue every day as only that would help calm the bees and restore order and peace. Both women again dropped to their knees and cried out on behalf of Sir Theo.

Together all of them toured every inch of the library that used to hold secrets and cleaned up all the dirt and oozy soot. Running to the fountain of living water often, they used it to wash away filth and corrupt communication and vile thoughts that did not align with the Ancient One. Now, every thought was under captivity and brought under the Lordship of the Heavenly Realm. This was quite the task; so much had been allowed to sit and fester and create crevices for the wicked ones to creep in and reside.

As they cleaned, any wayward thoughts or memories that would not be edifying, they locked away in the chests, holding them captive. The books were all lined up on the shelves neatly and in order, the papers and artifacts were cataloged and put in their assigned places to remain. Serenity reigned in the library of secrets. It had been a long time overdue, that was for sure.

The Overseer took one last penetrating look around all the floors of the library, looking for any possible remnants of Mr. Insidious's army or wayward thoughts. Satisfied with the peace that had settled over the library, He returned to the room of life that He resided in, the living room of the heart.

Chapter 10

Mr. Insidious was banished forever, but he knew that there were many others like him that would love to be able to cavort in Reba Jean's library. He went through the nether world looking for his replacement. He posted a "Help Wanted" sign by his camp and waited to see who was willing to do battle with the Ancient One and the Overseer. Oh, he would not tell them that they would have to fight; he did not want them to be leery of going to the library.

Gossip and Criticism came through. He signed them up; they could probably slip in through the cracks before Reba Jean or Lady Jane even realized they were already there. He gathered a root of bitterness from Bitterroot for them to take with them to plant. He waited some more to see who else he could recruit. He was careful to hide in the shadows so that they wouldn't see his fresh wounds from the Golden Swords. He knew his previous army was all licking their wounds and sulking in the dark. He did not want them to dissuade any new ones that would replace them. "Hmmm," he wondered, "Who would make a good captain of the next army?" His eyes glowed, and he went off in search of Discord.

Discord, Gossip, and Criticism along with Bitterroot, if he could convince them all to work together, they would make a great team. Oh, he literally howled with glee! He might not be able to go, but he could still direct from the nether realm. He did a quick prediction and checked the calendar from the library that he had copied. "Yes, that will be just the right time," he murmured to himself.

Reba Jean was scheduled to go to a Women's Conference at the end of the month. He knew when a bunch of so-called church women got together that invariably Gossip,

Criticism, and Discord were always beckoned forth and welcomed. He rubbed his conniving clawed hands together in full anticipation. He always played the long game; this was just going to be part of it.

Meanwhile, Reba Jean hugged Lady Jane, and they parted to their own tasks for the next little while. They both felt such a sense of peace and tranquility. Reba Jean went to church again and heard a message about Caleb claiming his promised mountain. She prayed for help for her husband and their family and finances. These were her mountains right now that needed victory over. She worked really hard at not watching anything on television. She was careful to distance herself from things that were not pleasing to the Lord. Vile thoughts or blasphemous suggestions were quickly defeated by earnest prayer, begging for forgiveness, mercy, and help from the fiery darts.

Her new job was very hard physically, and she prayed for strength, and it was granted. She was offered a second job and took that as a sign that the Lord was helping her financially. Reba Jean also took time to go back to a real prayer closet every morning and truly earnestly pray for her family and people. She felt a real settled peace come over her that she hadn't had in a very long while. She was on guard against the next onslaught of the evil ones. She was concerned about the Women's Conference but decided to pray about it instead.

Lady Jane twirled around in relief as the library settled down and began to function peacefully. The books stayed on their shelves, and the golden dust motes seemed to just permeate the air instead of hovering nearly in the rafters. The misty tendrils only seemed to dance around like wildflowers in a gentle breeze. The Ancient One often traced golden words of comfort in the air around her. She looked at the scar on her wrist and nearly cried at the thought of how close death had been. She mentally castigated herself for getting too familiar with sin and its ilk. Thinking about Mr. Insidious, she realized how Sinister he was. Then she did a little word game with that word… "Sin Astir" would be a good way to remember what that word was all about.

Later that night, the door to the library opened with a soft chime, and Reba Jean slipped into its peaceful interior. She had just received some hopeful news, and she needed to make a place for it in the library. She slipped down a hallway that had been bricked off as a path not taken. She touched the walled-in section and tried not to cry. Lady Jane came to see what was going on, and her expression was a myriad of emotions when she saw Reba Jean at THIS wall again.

What was behind this wall was a mess of emotions; even standing here caused a real stir in the books in the library. Reba Jean sank to the floor and began to cry in earnest. Behind this wall were the hopes and then the deep pain of losing three precious grandbabies in less than a year. She knew they were with Jesus, but she had steeled herself each time. Now, would the possible fourth one live down here or join its three siblings in Heaven? She would know more on Monday, but she found herself in that storm of emotions of past, present, and future.

Lady Jane sank to the floor and wrapped her arms around Reba Jean and added her tears with her Mistress's puddle of pain and promise. Reba Jean tried to pray but just didn't know how to hope or if she should. They heard misty tendrils dropping down and books opening around the library. This was probably not a good thing. Neither of them wanted to look at the books that were being written in or what was being thought by either of them. They were weary from the huge battle earlier in the day and felt they had no strength to even control their own thoughts.

The misty tendrils stopped almost suddenly, and a hush fell over the library. The women almost didn't notice, then the pages of the Ancient One could be heard flipping open, and soon the books were astir again. This time, the Ancient One was editing the thoughts that had been written down. Reba Jean realized she had been subconsciously praying for help. She relaxed a bit, reached up and touched the bricks on the wall, wondering if they appeared a bit more transparent or if the Lord would remove them, and they would walk down this hallway soon planning for a grandbaby.

With a prayer and a swallowed sob, she hugged Lady Jane and left the library to try to get some sleep. The next few days were going to be a hodge-podge of thoughts and emotions, she was sure. Lady Jane was left to wander and wonder; this had felt unexpected, and she was unsure how things would go this time around. Lady Jane sighed, "Oh Lord Rabboni, please don't let this cause evil to come into this library yet again."

Reba Jean spent the weekend exhausted both physically and emotionally. She was thankful for her renewed vigil in the prayer closet; it felt like that missing piece had been located, and things were stronger than they had been in recent months. She continued to monitor her thoughts and was appalled by how easy it was to think something that was not pleasing to the Lord. Some thoughts that came her way felt like outward attacks; she literally would flinch when they came into her mind. How could she protect herself from them even entering; she prayed about this often.

She dreamed a disgusting dream and was appalled at what her subconscious had brought forth while she was asleep. She had to find a way to keep her dreams sweet. She knew dreams could draw on anything the mind was still trying to process, but she needed to heal what seemed like a fractured mind. Yes, she knew her mind was not saved, but she was horrified at what it would concoct and put together while she was imprisoned by sleep.

Reba Jean was scared to see if those books had somehow been unlocked and re-opened in the library. Some secrets did not need to see the light of day, neither should they even be made manifest in any way, shape, or form. *"Create in me a clean heart O God; and renew a right spirit within me,"* she breathed a prayer from a Psalm.

Thoughts of the upcoming Women's Conference frustrated her; she had committed herself to go, but she was afraid it would be a mental disaster or a spiritual disappointment for her. She needed to pray hard for this conference and for all those who were going to be there. She wanted a spiritual renewal, not a digress in her walk with the Lord.

Mr. Insidious decided to send a scout out just to see what might be going on in the aftermath of that battle. He needed to know if he needed more recruits. He decided to send Doubtful to go check in on the women. He wasn't aware of all that was going on; it wasn't like he was omniscient, even if he wanted them to think he was.

Doubtful slipped out of the nether world and began sniffing around Reba Jean. He whispered to her every once in a while, just little questions here and there. This was so much fun; he didn't have to do anything but just ask her little things or make comments that would have her thinking in a different direction. If he could just take her mind off of trusting God, then mission accomplished!

Reba Jean wasn't aware that she had Doubtful hounding her, but she knew she was going to have a mess in the library again if she did not get her thoughts under control. She went to church and worshipped the Lord almost in desperation. Sunday afternoon, she contacted a publisher for her book, and then she realized that Doubtful was in high gear.

She would have to proofread this book of hers; she had already decided to eliminate a possible reoccurring character. She hadn't killed off any characters in the book yet and here she was about to do what she despised others for doing. She doubted that the book was worth publishing or even letting others read it. When it was just a possibility of anonymity, she felt more secure, but this publisher was someone she knew. Reba Jean felt panic set in, and she felt very anxious.

Doubtful sent a message back to Mr. Insidious; he had started the process ahead of the conference. He recommended though that Anxiety would be a great asset to their cause. He could cause doubt, but Anxiety could do real damage without lifting more than a finger. This was great news to Mr. Insidious, and he quickly dispatched Anxiety from his current mission and sent him to wreak havoc with Reba Jean. He anticipated that the battle was over before the Women's Conference was even upon them.

What would Reba Jean do? Her friend Mardie had remonstrated her to tell it like it is and not worry about the truth hurting people. Reba Jean, however, didn't think that every secret needed to be aired like dirty laundry. As she prepared her lecture for the weekly meeting with the fledgling librarians, she came across Scripture that applied to her own situation.

"Search me, O God, and know my heart: try me and know my thoughts: And see if there be any wicked way in me, and lead me in the way everlasting." Then a phrase she had included in her lecture notes, jumped out at her. "Don't undo in doubt, what you did in faith!" She asked the Lord to calm her doubts and fears and to soothe her anxiety. God had given her this book, whatever His will would be concerning it, she just had to finish writing it. "Oh Lord," she prayed, "let this book be pleasing in Your sight; have Your will and way in it."

Reba Jean eliminated the thought of adding that extra character to her storyline and changed some wording and character naming in her storyline. She was really intimidated now about editing anything. She felt the anxiety rush in on her; she wondered how all this was affecting Lady Jane and the library. All these secrets! Less than five people knew she was writing a book, and even fewer than that knew about the library. She knew everyone had a library of secrets, but she doubted that many of them realized they could truly guard their thoughts. Mental health was such an increasing problem in the past few years, or maybe it had always been, but it was taboo to talk about. It was time to check on Lady Jane.

Chapter 11

Lady Jane alternated between watching storm clouds brew and shivering as tangible snatches of dread descended here and there. What was going on with Reba Jean? Shivering, she went to check the library books scattered around to get a sense of what was astir. The air was thick in here, and she felt goosebumps come upon her arms. Clutching her middle in panic, she watched someone she had thought was a friend seemingly disappear off the pages of the open book. She remembered how other friends had been relegated to just memories as well. So used to the library and its jumbled ways, she failed to even realize that the open book was the actual book that Reba Jean was trying to write about the library. The significance of this particular book was completely unnoticed.

Running over to her communication console, a quick message was sent to Lady Constance. It was a relief to have someone who understood the mess this library always seemed to get into. Lady Jane was slightly comforted by the love that Lady Constance showed her even while she was fighting her own battles. They were comrades in arms, fighting for the safety and sanity of their libraries.

Out of the corner of her eye, she thought she noticed two odd creatures lurking in the shadows. One looked like a hound dog, but she did not think that Reba Jean had any dogs, much less allowed them in the library! The other creature was more like a hedgehog in appearance. His glowing eyes, however, gave her the creeps. She felt panic come over her as she tried to watch him surreptitiously.

Reba Jean shivered and felt an anxious knot in the pit of her stomach form. It just felt like everything was getting out of control the more she tried to control it. She couldn't seem to control her dreams, even in the middle of praying, vile thoughts would leap out, and she still struggled with how to deal with people.

She even felt panic about what would happen when the book was finished; it had become her faithful friend waiting for her. She was crazy to give life to an inanimate object. The only living book was the Bible, and here she was, almost anthropomorphizing a measly, little, old, unpublished book.

Doubtful and Anxiety swirled around Reba Jean's head whispering to her, sometimes running claw-like fingers down her arm in pseudo comfort. They just wanted her to think like they did. She was a nobody, and the more she realized that the easier it would be for them to fracture her sensibilities. Minds were very fragile, and hers was still not healed from all the trauma of yesteryears. She had dug up secrets in hopes of vindication and justification, and instead, had just caused more wounds to herself.

Reba Jean turned on the orchestrated hymns hoping to calm her nerves and anxious mind. She was so very tired, and there was still so much to do today. Opening to her devotions in 2 Kings 12, she was struck by how applicable this chapter was to her. So much had been given to repair the breaches in the walls of her mind, and yet, the repair work had not been finished.

Lady Jane ran to the Ancient One sitting on the rugged wooden table. She needed comfort from the Overseer, maybe the Golden Sword would be there to defend her if those creatures came out of the shadows. Why were there shadows anyway in the library? Hearing the door whoosh open, she shrank at the foot of the table hugging it. Reba Jean surveyed the tossed books, the dark storm clouds brewing overhead, and the shadows chasing each other through the aisles. She felt goosebumps multiply on her flesh, and she choked on a sudden feeling of panic in her throat.

With a look of dismay at the uneasiness surrounding her, Reba Jean realized she had caused this chaos, or at least allowed it to happen. Where was Lady Jane? Rubbing the gooseflesh on her arms, she could faintly hear the hymns, why was the sound so low up in here? Trying to shake off that feeling of panic, she glanced at the walled-in hallway that she had visited the other night. It was still walled up, and seemed to have claw marks on some of the bricks. Her eyes widened; did she have creatures from the nether world in here again? Oh, where was Lady Jane?

Lady Jane did not know who else was in the library; she did not want to know. She just wanted to be comforted; her whole body felt like it was going to shatter. She hated it when it was like this. She started banging her head against the table and began to moan. Where was the Overseer, where was Lord Rabboni? "Oh, King Abba, please forgive me; I am so unworthy to be here." She withdrew inside herself.

Doubtful and Anxiety began to cavort through the aisles; it was working! They brushed against Reba Jean but did not want to really alert her to their presence. Instead, they focused on Lady Jane; if they could cause her to shatter, then Reba Jean would be easy prey to their devices. Oh, Mr. Insidious would be so proud of them. They danced even closer to Lady Jane whispering doubts and anxious ideas to her as she clung to the table leg.

Reba Jean began to forget why she was even in the library; the noise of the books and the odd shadows began to seem normal to her. Her eyes glazed over, and she stopped in mid-stride and stared off into nothing. She was truly lost in her thoughts. Thoughts concerning her book seemed almost laughable; who did she think she was to be writing a book? Even much less, expecting any editor or publisher to distribute it to the masses. No, they would think it was childish and mindless drivel. Oh, she could use big words, but it was just a bunch of gobbledygook. She sat down on the floor and felt her head start to swim. Her thoughts were just misfired synapses, and she looked up to actually see frayed wires dangling over her head sparking in short circuit.

The two creatures didn't dare leave, but oh, how they wished Mr. Insidious could see how well his plan was working. They silently howled in unholy glee. Reba Jean and Lady Jane were putty in their well-trained hands. Lady Jane was hugging the table of the very Thing that could comfort her, and yet she was not receiving any comfort. This was just amazing; they did not think they had power over the Ancient One, but maybe they did after all!

Reba Jean glanced at her watch and realized that she would need to get to work. The library would have to be left to its own devices for a while. She vaguely noticed cracks forming in the walls; she would have to repair them some time or the whole place would fall in on itself. Her head felt heavy with thoughts, and yet she couldn't seem to latch onto them or exert control over them. All her holier-than-thou thoughts paraded before her, dancing like little minions onto the pages of open books waiting to record every thought she had.

She detached herself from what was happening in the library, gathered her skirts under her, and exited much the same way she had arrived. Lady Jane had the Ancient One; she would be fine. She had to just get some energy to go to work and try to keep it together. She would hope the phone call later today would relieve some of the anxiety and not compound it. She felt on the verge of tears again, and the anxious knot in her stomach was still there. Inhaling, Reba Jean set about pulling her last shred of sanity together to try to make it through the day. She had a nagging thought that she needed to repair the breaches in the walls of her mind but did not seem to know how to go about it. She stifled an inward scream and tried to find some resolve to make it through the day.

She had obviously not spent enough time in her prayer closet, she caught a glimpse of her countenance in a reflection, and it almost scared her. She saw a very unflattering look about her that reminded her of her mother. She had vowed not to be like her, including how she handled situations. Was she becoming like her mother? Was it because of the autistic gene? Was it inevitable? All these years of fighting against it, working so hard not to let it control her, had she just wasted years of energy?

Driving to work, she tried to pray but felt like it was just bubbles of air bursting over her head. She wanted so much to have a good day at work, but she was already swimming in over her head with all the thoughts in her mind.

As she drove half listening to the Christian radio station, a statement from a preacher grabbed her attention. He quoted from John 14:27, but what he expounded reached into the inner recesses of her heart. She meditated on it all day. "Peace I leave with you, my peace I GIVE unto you: not as the world giveth,

GIVE I unto you. Let not your heart be troubled, neither let it be afraid."

She had often said that you couldn't have the peace of God until you were at peace with God. This verse said that God's peace was a gift that HE gives to you. It has nothing to do with your level of righteousness. The preacher she listened to on the way home from a hard but good day at work, reminded her to keep the proper perspective of herself.

After supper, she slipped up to the library to truly repair the breaches that had appeared in such a quick interval. The shadows were still lingering, the wires still fritzing, and she found Lady Jane huddled in a moaning heap. She ignored the goosebumps, but the hair on the back of her neck was all a tingle.

She determinedly opened the Ancient One to John 14:27 and began to read aloud. Golden strands sang out softly, forming the shape of a gift box, and Reba Jean set the gift of peace on Lady Jane's lap. Lady Jane realized that King Abba had given her a gift, and it was based on His Word, not on her feelings. Faith over feelings—both women had forgotten that very important principle.

Reba Jean reached up and caught a few golden dust motes in her hand, dipping them into the box and bringing her hand back up to find it covered with a beautiful soothing oil. She caught Lady Jane's hands and rubbed the oil of gladness over them. It might not be the warm fuzzies, but the peace of God was a gift worth feeling.

Lady Jane felt the peace that now she realized she had been given from the beginning. It was time to conquer the shadows in the library and seal up any breaches. Together, they strolled down the aisles, replaced books, swept away shadows, and tidied up the beautiful interior of the library that had been marred by battles and enemy interference. They passed by Sir Theo's library, and she let the peace waft into his library. He, too, needed peace from God; it might not solve the issues, but it would be a salve to him. They listened as the angry bees settled down into a soft hum that sounded like "There Will be Peace in the Valley."

They found themselves in front of the brick wall that Reba Jean had been crying at just a few hours earlier. With the box of peace, they dipped their fingers in the oil and wiped the bricks with the oil of gladness and peace. Three of the bricks turned golden, and a fourth brick became a translucent crystal. The wall was still there, but time would tell what God had planned for the hallway beyond.

Doubtful and Anxiety had to dodge those golden dust motes and duck away from the beautiful light that permeated the library as the Ancient One and the gift box of Peace were now in control. Mr. Insidious thought he was in control, but if he found out about this, the two rapscallions would be in serious trouble. They ducked in and out of aisles, looking for some place they could hide undetected. It was then that they noticed the breaches were being sealed shut! How were they going to get out? How would they get back in if they did leave?

They were feeling their own doubts and anxiety; soon, they turned on each other, fighting to feel superior and in control. This was the scene when Lady Jane and Reba Jean turned an outside corner by the farthest wall. They had come to inspect it for any hidden cracks or crevices. Reba Jean held out her hand and the Golden Sword appeared instantly. She took a mighty swing; her momentum caused her to lose her hold on the gift box. The sword swung, the oil and the box of peace all connected with the two minions of the nether world, and the vermin were instantly dissolved into an oozy puddle. With a quick thrust of the Sword, Reba Jean stuck it into the puddle and the ooze was dispatched into the nether world.

Doubtful and Anxiety found themselves back into the sulfurous underworld that they had called headquarters since they were created. They immediately attacked each other upon sight, hoping to wound the other sufficiently that Mr. Insidious would think they had survived an enormous battle. Watching from a distance was the young apprentice, Insecurity. He watched Doubtful and Anxiety for a few minutes and slithered off to notify Mr. Insidious of their return.

He saw through the lies and deceit, enough to realize that his attempts to control the library from the outside had failed at least at this time. However, he eyed Insecurity and began to consider a different tactic. Insecurity might only be an apprentice, but maybe he could do even more harm as he did not look as threatening. Mr. Insidious sat down to plot his next move with Insecurity listening intently and even getting to add his own slimy perspective.

Doubtful and Anxiety were demoted to spend some time in retraining as foot soldiers for the Evil Lord of the Underworld. They teamed up with Disgruntled and Frustration and secretly plotted their own revenge on Reba Jean and that simpering Lady Jane.

Reba Jean and Lady Jane finished their tour of the library and listened to the peace that was reigning finally. It was so peaceful you actually could feel it.

They settled down in Lady Jane's inner sanctum and humming softly began watching the tendrils draw pictures of babies, puppies, cats, flowers, and musical notes. Reba Jean felt her eyes closing, and she knew it was time for her to go to bed. She hugged Lady Jane and reminded her to read John 14 at any time she felt like something was wrong in the library.

Reba Jean walked slowly to the door of the library, soaking in the peace, and hoping it would go with her as she went down to the living room. Then, she remembered it was from God and nothing could separate her from the love of God. She drew her heart closer to the Lord, asking Him to help her dreams be sweet and clean and pleasing to Him.

Stuffing down the anxious doubts, she commanded herself to trust God that He would do what was best for their family. God would also have His perfect will concerning the book she was writing. She spent some time praying and thanking the Lord for His peace and love that had strengthened her through this day.

She felt the words of another verse during the day and had to look it up to refresh her memory. She lost track of what she was looking for when she landed in Psalms 119, and she let the precious Words seep into her soul. The verse nudged her again, and she found it in Psalm 139:23 "Search me, O God, and know my heart; try me, and know my thoughts: And see if there be any wicked way in me, and lead me in the way everlasting."

Reba Jean determined to have good dreams, so she went to bed praying for God to search her and clean her thoughts and heart from any wicked way. The Lord just wanted her to trust Him. She needed to practice that trust in every aspect of her life.

After a few more busy, exhausting days, it was time to check in on Lady Jane and the library. What secrets would it share? Was Lady Jane handling her end of the workload? What sort of evil minions were swirling around just looking for the slimmest opportunity to launch an assault on the fragility of the sanity of those two women? Reba Jean had all these questions and more, yet was reluctant to find out what the answers would be. Keeping thoughts captive was exhausting and quite a battle.

Meanwhile, Insecurity decided to prove his mettle by finding his own little band of cohorts, and they commenced to slink into the middle world. Insecurity knew that an outright assault was not the best strategy. Instead, he just had to affect those around Reba Jean. With her empathic tendencies, she would start feeling insecure and frustrated through everyone else around her. Insecurity loved this way of getting his mission accomplished. Then Blame, Guilt, and Resentment could work their wiles on the unsuspecting target.

This became a very effective strategy, one that even Reba Jean noticed but didn't seem to know how to fight against. Too busy and way too tired to do anything but complain about it seemed to be the end result. Insecurity could just feel a promotion to higher ranks in his grasp. Reba Jean had already been worn down by Doubtful and Anxiety, but he would reap their results!

"I Need Thee, Every Hour" was playing on the sound system; it had become almost an anthem to Reba Jean these days. It was time to inspect the library and put things in order if there were any issues. Visiting that certain hallway from earlier was also necessary.

Distracted by a phone call, these plans were again delayed.

Reba Jean had second thoughts about the Women's Conference, and the idea of being around people as much as she had been and would be in the next few weeks was beginning to irritate her. Already it was starting to look like she would say something mean or stupid without thinking before this month was over. Even her book had seemed to hit a snag for a few days. Writer's block had not been an issue all this time. There was definitely something going on that needed fixing, or did it?

Chapter 12

Feeling cranky but determined, up the steps to the library she strode. With every intent of being serene, the door still managed to swing open violently, crashing into the wall behind it. The chime sounded harsh, and immediate thoughts of disabling it caused it to stop with a whine. This idea of things being produced by her thoughts gave her a moment of pride and power. Then she stopped when she caught a glimpse of the fountain in the middle of the atrium. It had not been in the atrium before, but it seemed the perfect spot for it. Her emotions were swinging like a proverbial pendulum. Not seeing Lady Jane, even though her entrance had been very noisy, she decided to venture to the side hallway alone.

Lady Jane heard the door crash open but chose not to investigate. The abrupt whine of the door chime being cut off was interesting to note, though. She sat and stared at all the tendrils jumping up and down like yo-yos that couldn't make up their mind. Only certain books were open; at least it wasn't a total mess. It wasn't her fault if Reba Jean couldn't make up her mind what she was thinking about, was it?

Lady Jane folded her arms and sat in her chair with a resolute expression fixed on her features. Soothing hymns from the sound system could be heard if one was paying attention to them. Distraction and Frustration seemed to be running around unnoticed. Lady Jane slumped back and let her focus fade into nothing.

Creeping down the hallway, Reba Jean noticed that the brick wall with the three golden bricks seemed to be more translucent, and the crystal brick was glowing like a diamond in the sunlight streaming through the windows overhead. Sitting down next to the wall, she felt it move against her weight. Was it possible that it could be torn down? She pushed on the wall, and it moved back five feet; her eyes widened. Golden dust motes filtered down and gently removed the three golden bricks forming them into three golden tiles on the floor in front of the wall. The crystal brick was then placed in the middle of the translucent wall. This was a wall of hope; maybe the Lord would allow this baby to live here on earth with its family.

Reba Jean knelt next to the three golden tiles and caressed them with her shaking fingers. A mixture of closure and mourning seemed to finally seep out of her more than in previous months. Misty tendrils slid some books over to her and started to write and draw pictures, only to be smeared before they were finished. What was this? Not even her thoughts were able to be recorded correctly. Feelings of unworthiness, shame, and insecurity flooded her mind.

Holding her head between her hands, she slumped to the floor in a defeated heap. She just wanted to run away and hide, go to the ocean or the mountains or something, just to get away from it all. So many people, so many expectations, and living for Christ seemed impossible. What sort of Christian was she anyway? It was Easter weekend, and she felt the overwhelming weight of her sin upon her.

Hearing a soft, comforting rustle of pages, she was pulled from her mental anguish to hear the Ancient One beckoning her. It had opened to Galatians 2:20, and after she read it, then it flipped a couple of golden pages to Philippians 4:13. Gulping back a lump in her throat, she regained a proper perspective. Writing the book, working, being a wife, mother, maybe grandmother, and child of God all hinged on the Lord's strength, not her own.

Standing up and stretching to release the tension, she went looking for Lady Jane. The poor dear looked lost and very fragile in her position on the chair. Refusing to even look at

Reba Jean, she stayed slumped, almost in a defensive position. She knew her dreams hadn't been horrible since she had started praying hard for peaceful sleep each night. What was wrong with Lady Jane?

Reba Jean dipped her skirt hem into the fountain of living water and gently wiped Lady Jane's brow. The water seemed to soak straight into her pores, and she lifted her head as life seemed to fill her empty eyes. Looking at Reba Jean, she slowly let her arms drop to her sides as the strength of the Word of King Abba and Lord Rabboni seeped into her being. Staring at each other, reading each other's thoughts, they silently apologized to each other.

Staring at the sun rays flowing down from the windows above, Reba Jean looked around and then stopped, and with a grin, she thought a spiral staircase into place. Giggling, she grabbed Lady Jane by the hand, and together they raced up the staircase to look out the beautiful agate-colored windows. Oh, what a beautiful world there was to see! Birds swinging on flower baskets, hummingbirds flitting around the feeders, and the willow tree rustling in the breeze. Oh, what a beautiful world Reba Jean lived in! Lady Jane felt love and peace flow through her and the library around her. Serenity was once again in place, and feelings of frustration and insecurity were abated for now.

Reba Jean left Lady Jane staring out the windows, and she wandered back down the stairs to meander along the aisles. Memory Lane had recently been visited but was not a mess. The wall of hope was gleaming but still intact. Soft hymns playing through the sound system were just the perfect dreamy touch to the now serene atmosphere. Misty tendrils dropped down to draw bucolic scenes of artwork in some of the books, and Lady Jane could be heard whispering words of thanksgiving to Lord Rabboni for His peace and strength.

Thinking about peace, Reba Jean wandered over to the Ancient One and flipped its pages again to John 14. Then being reminded that it was Easter weekend, the pages seemed to redirect her to the Easter Story. She sobbed inwardly as she was reminded that this peace was a real gift from her Savior.

There was a pause in the music, and she could hear clocks ticking around her. It was time to be strong in the Lord and in the power of His might. She checked the condition of her armor; she had to wear it constantly because the attacks of the Evil One were constant and seemingly out of the blue. The Golden Sword responded to her summons, and she stood straight and tall ready to face the insecurities of the day.

She blew a kiss to Lady Jane who was daydreaming out the windows at the top of the newly carved balustrade. The library was going to be just fine as long as they kept their perspective on Christ and not on themselves. This day, a couple of thousand years ago, at this time of day, Jesus Christ was thinking of me!

"Oh Lord, You alone are worthy of praise, honor, and glory for Your supreme sacrifice for my sins. Thank You, Lord, for saving a wretch like me."

Lady Jane felt the strength wrap its arms around her, and even though Reba Jean was exiting the library, the prayer she had breathed seemed to come alive in the confines of the library. "Nearer my God to Thee" began to play over the sound system; it was as if the very presence of the whole Royal Trinity was there at that moment. Lady Jane dropped to her knees and worshipped with all her being.

Reba Jean, feeling resolved and at peace, descended to the kitchen to think about lunch. Her thoughts were never far from what Jesus must have been going through at this particular time so many years ago. He was probably already descending to hell to preach to the captives there. Sunday was coming! Lunch was cooking, and she was working on more of her novel. Feelings of insecurity were being brushed away even though they kept swirling like pesky mosquitoes. It was up to God if this book was ever going to be read by anyone. Writing it was just what she was supposed to do, the rest would happen when God willed it to happen.

The weight of frustration and insecurity had lessened for a time; maybe things would be able to be accomplished more efficiently without all the extra second guessing. Writing was more than a new hobby. It was more than cathartic; it had become an avenue to gauge what she was thinking and how she was thinking. Did her thoughts line up with the truth of God's Word? It was easy to tell others what to do and how to think, but to actually put it into practice personally was much more difficult.

Six months had passed, and one young librarian was about to graduate from the course. She would receive her certification next week; then, she would be in charge of keeping her library in order. Many had graduated, but few seemed to thrive.

Just like reading books, living for the Lord often seemed to be rare and going out of style these days. Then a reminder from the devotions in 1 Kings came to mind; no, there was nothing new under the sun. Living for the Lord was not being mass-produced, but it was still being practiced by a remnant who had not given in to the worship of the world.

It felt like hypocrisy sometimes, she contemplated. She could teach the truth of God's Word to others, but her own tendency to have wicked thoughts often made her feel like a Pharisee. At times, she suspected that her desire to be isolated came not from some avoidant personality disorder but from her knowledge of her own spiritual failures. She couldn't be a stumbling block if she wasn't around anyone, right? NO, she remonstrated herself; her lack of presence might be the cause for someone to stumble.

God had made it clear to her a couple of years ago that He wanted to use her past, her wounds, her upbringing to help others who also felt unloved and unwanted. Too many people mistook a transformed life for one that had never had problems or sin. She had been through so much, even if just in her mind at times, yet God wanted her mess to be His message. It was evident that her past connected with others who felt like victims, and thus it was possible to see that there was a purpose for it making all the trauma worthwhile.

"Only what is done for Christ will last" rang in her thoughts as she sat there contemplating what the Lord had done in her life over the last few decades. It wasn't about being "holier than thou," but being holier than before. The comparison chart had been ripped down; now, she just needed to think about things that brought her closer to the Lord.

The thought of being around all the people that were prone to gossip, murmur, complain, and be conceited threatened to overwhelm Reba Jean again. She inhaled deeply and clung to the strength and peace that she had received that morning. She tamped down any wayward thoughts and pushed back against the insecurity.

That little, irritating minion was working hard to be effective in this onslaught before the Women's Conference. He did not have access to the library directly, but he just kept whispering and suggesting things. He began to believe that he had more right to be in the library than Doubtful and Anxiety. What a mess of failure they had been. It was obvious that his method of attacking through others was doing more damage than any other foot soldiers of the lord of the dark realm. Looking at his name branded on his chest, he noticed that the two I's glowed a burnt orange color. Oh yes, pride was working on him, fashioning him into a loyal foot soldier. He swelled up and preened a little bit more than before.

Insecurity came out of himself for a second to take stock of the situation. He need not get too carried away; he still had the best strategy, in his opinion. Snickering, he noticed the blemishes on Reba Jean's face and her straggly hair. Yes, calling her out about her appearance and how her stress and eating habits were making her even more unattractive might just work.

Reba Jean felt restless and was getting lost in her thoughts. That wouldn't help Lady Jane if all the peace of the morning was wrecked by her discontentment. It was time to scrub the bathroom; that might help her get a proper perspective on her wayward thoughts. Nothing is as humbling or allegorical as cleaning a bathroom when one needed a proper perspective. Stretching to release pent-up frustration and tension, she saved her manuscript and gritted her teeth for the task ahead.

There! Bathrooms conquered, dishes finished, laundry put away, more loads in the machine. Catching a ghastly reflection in the mirror that was being wiped clean, Reba Jean doggedly applied coconut oil to the blemishes that had popped up on her face. Cleaning with fierce determination, the thought popped into her mind that she hadn't even remembered to prepare the upcoming lecture for the itinerant librarians. Frustration set in at her lapse of memory then calmed down; it was evident that only God gives the lesson plans, and He just hadn't done that yet. That used to bother her need for security, control, and planning, now it was just a matter of trust and obedience. He knew what was meant to be said; it was under His control and timing. Relaxing, she forced herself to expend that frustration of energy into doing the tasks that she really despised completing fully. As usual, a spiritual application was often found in most things she saw or did.

After her attack on the housework that had been neglected most of the week due to her long hours at her job, she sat back down to write more in her book. She had a self-imposed deadline, and she was woefully behind on where she ought to be. She laughed at herself scornfully; she just hoped the editor wouldn't make her change a whole lot of stuff. She was aware that her grammar probably wasn't even up to the standards that she imposed on others. If the publisher she had spoken with had even gotten this far, he was probably fixing to send her into counseling. Yes, this book was in the category of truth is stranger than fiction. She sought comfort in the fact that only a handful of people knew she was writing a book. Those who knew were supportive at least, but she doubted any of them would read it. In fact, Mardie was waiting for it to be read to her!

If it was read to her husband, he would fall asleep; he always did when she talked too long. She contemplated the use of a pseudonym again. Would the publisher let her? Was it deceitful to use a pen name? She needed to just discuss it with them. Scrolling through social media brought a laugh to her when she read a friend's post and the comments encouraged that friend to write a book. Here she was, actually writing one unbeknownst to the world at large.

It was so easy to feel insecure about everything, so many questions, but only time would have the answers. Realizing that she was probably causing a yo-yo affect upstairs in the library, she calmed down and tried not to think. That was laughable too; she usually had three trains of thought going down the track, and one was always fixing to derail. Sipping her Ginger Ale, she felt relief that a lot of the day's tasks were finally finished. They had seemed so overwhelming and unable to be completed before they were even started; now, here she was, able to rejoice that they were finished. Surely there was yet a spiritual application in that scenario. How often do we think that living for the Lord is impossible and overwhelming due to our carnal nature and lazy tendencies until we actually make ourselves do it in the power of the Holy Ghost, then we look back and wonder why it was so hard.

Still not knowing what her next lecture topic was going to be, she decided not to worry about it. Ticking off the mental checklist, she decided to check on the laundry and take a few minutes to thank the Lord for helping her do what seemed impossible. "Oh Lord, You have blessed me with an education, an intelligence, and a vivid imagination, please help me to use all of these for Your honor and glory..." she found herself praying instead. Hmmm, now that was interesting, her thought had been on her material blessings, but her mind was on a different topic for giving thanks.

She needed to get through just two hours of a party tomorrow, then Easter Sunday needed to be all about Jesus, not fashion and family. Monday she would give her lecture and the final exam for the graduating student. Monday night was the certification ceremony for that student and reception with family, faculty, and friends. She had no idea what she was going to be working doing next week, but she would just have to take it all one day at a time. The lyrics of a song by that same title swung into her mind... She giggled. Yes, her mental trains were going a mile a minute in all sorts of random directions. No one would know if she was having a stroke or not, this was all so normal for her.

Maybe it was like having ADHD after all, who knew? She knew how to be very quiet on the outside, but her mind was rarely quiet or still, and it would bounce from topic to topic like a ping pong ball on steroids. She found it interesting that the Bible spoke of a transformed mind, but never said it was to be a still, quiet mind... did it? She would need to look that up; oh yes "Thou wilt keep him in perfect peace, whose mind is stayed on Thee..." she quoted to herself. Well, based on that paraphrase my mind should be at peace... Does that mean it needs to be quiet all the time? She was in real trouble if it meant that her mind needed to be sedated to be tranquil. Those words brought up thoughts of sedation and tranquilizer, and she burst out laughing at herself.

Still giggling, she ran up the stairs to the library; she just had to check to see if there were yo-yos, derailed trains, or ping pong balls flying around. If she thought it, it was either happening up there or at least drawn in a book somewhere. She needed to get Lady Jane a helmet if this kept up. Opening the door carefully, prepared to duck flying objects, she peeked into the library.

Lady Jane was standing in the middle of the atrium with a silly expression on her face. "You're crazy, Reba Jean... you know that, right?" Lady Jane chortled. "I think you need to send me on a vacation, where there is peace and quiet." They both giggled and scooped up ping pong balls, rolled up yo-yos, and turned off the toy train sets that were speeding around newly laid tracks down the hallways.

Crazy or not, this looked much more fun to be in compared to when that sinister creature was allowed in to wreak havoc. Striking a pose, Lady Jane raised her finger and intoned "A mind is a terrible thing to waste," and then collapsed in a heap on the floor giggling.

"Pshaw," exclaimed Reba Jean, "there is no waste here, everything is recycled into something else." Together they stretched out on their backs listening to the hymns filtering in on the sound system, the dust motes dancing merrily in the sunshine, and the misty tendrils all a quiver waiting for the next thought to form itself under their design.

They both exhaled sighs of contentment in unison and tried to soak in the peace and tranquility that still permeated the library. No thoughts of secrets or past scars or shame came to haunt them as they lay there basking in the gift of peace. Catching a glimpse of a blue butterfly fluttering around, Lady Jane pointed it out to Reba Jean. There had been a time when they thought that little blue gem was going to be turned into a bat or some sort of nefarious varmint. The arrival of the Overseer had changed all of that.

Hearts united in thanksgiving and praise, the two women closed their eyes in prayer and praise to Lord Rabboni for all they had been brought through in just a few short days. Opening their eyes, Reba Jean thought some hummingbirds and flowers would be beautiful adornments to the library, so she waved the tendrils into action. It was almost Easter; maybe there should be a huge bouquet of Easter lilies in the Atrium and at the foot of the rugged table holding the Ancient One.

Feeling the beauty of spring, they watched lovely patches of flowers bloom up in areas around the library, and you could almost smell their heady scents. The two women linked arms and walked around the library touching books and shelves and rearranging artifacts. They draped beautiful purple tapestry over the locked chests and breathed a prayer as they walked past Sir Theo's library entrance. Down the hallway of hope, they carried a bouquet of white roses and laid them on the golden tiles.

Finding another hallway, they walked down to the brick wall at its end and laid a bouquet of yellow roses in honor of Momma of the Glen, who had been in Heaven with Lord Rabboni these almost thirteen years. Feeling a teary ball form in her throat, Reba Jean swallowed it back and refused to keep mourning the loss of her beloved mother-in-love.

"Holy, Holy, Holy" once again played over the sound system; they both stopped still and let the song of worship flood over them. Everything came to a standstill and a holy hush fell over the library. They both longed for it to be like this all the time. The stillness was so strong they felt like crying, it seemed almost alive. It was! The Overseer had arrived during their moments of praise and worship to Lord Rabboni. He watched as they soaked in the gift of peace into their hearts and minds. This was why He had been sent, to remind them Who it was all about. Only the strands of sacred music could be heard. They didn't need to run away to achieve this mental peace of mind; they just needed to keep their minds on Christ. He could truly help them, heal them, and hold them if only they would let Him.

Chapter 13

Insecurity and his friends felt like they had run into a brick wall at warp speed. The assault had been going just fine. What was this? He had scorned and scoffed at Doubtful and Anxiety and their crew, but he had never run into the Overseer before. After all, he was just an apprentice learning through observation and hadn't really been in battle with the Heavenly forces yet.

They tried to attack again, only to be stopped with such force that they found themselves licking their wounds. Looking at each other, they were confounded at this turn of events. Time to regroup; maybe it was time to find another way around this celestial roadblock in their path to mental destruction. Hoping that their evil overlords wouldn't find out about this, they huddled together to plot another scheme.

Mr. Insidious sat back on his haunches and watched from a distance. He wasn't too worried about this visit from the Overseer; he knew from experience it wouldn't last. Those two silly women always fell prey to his schemes before they even realized it. Insecurity was doing just fine weaving in and out among friends, family, and associates; he could stay on the job a while longer. That Women's Conference was still coming up; he knew that would be the clincher. Reba Jean might even be aware of his use of Insecurity, but she wasn't impervious to his effect on her.

He consulted his notes. Oh yes, the anniversary gift, that was a way to trip her up. He sent a scout to Insecurity to suggest that particular avenue of worming his way through the enemy lines. Insecurity understood that he was being watched but that so far, he had the support of the overlords. He puffed up with pride again at this commendation from his superior.

Looking around, he spied Worry and Anxiety coming to join his ranks. Just as long as they knew he was the one in charge, they could help him, but they had better not claim the accolades for a job well done. It was every minion for himself, as far as he was concerned.

Watching Reba Jean settle back down to write more in her book, he whispered around her. She didn't seem to be listening until he saw her touch one of her facial blemishes. Ahh, yes, the golden-bricked wall seems to have been weakened. He whispered some more questions and suppositions in the air around her and watched them linger. He knew they would linger there until she banished them. He felt his wounds ache and decided to just take it slow and easy; just the little skirmishes could win the battle.

Mr. Insidious knew that Insecurity was the right imp for the job; he watched him resume his sly attack on Reba Jean and felt unholy glee well up inside of him. The Overseer was not always going to stop their attacks unless Reba Jean let Him. The fact that she did not seem to allow the Overseer to have complete control was his happy foothold to hang onto. If he could get her to lose her sanity or her testimony, then she would be unusable by the celestial realm, and he could torment her any time he desired. Lady Jane was just an avatar of the library of the mind, she was really just imaginary, but oh did he like vain imaginations!

Mr. Insidious rolled back on his haunches, squinted his glowing eyes, and watched the next few days unfold. There was much that still could be accomplished for the evil lord of the Dark Realm. Maybe, if Reba Jean was important enough of a victim, he would get promoted for his meddling ways in her life and mind.

Reba Jean fingered the blemishes on her face and scowled. She was so sensitive about her appearance, but adding unsightly teenaged blemishes was like adding salt to an open wound. She got up to check the mail and rub more coconut oil on her face. Already the moments of peace in the library seemed but a distant memory even though it had happened just moments earlier.

Insecurity had a wild urge which emboldened him to attempt a stronger approach to his scheme. He disguised himself as a Concern and Care team member and knocked on the door of the library. Lady Jane wasn't used to someone knocking on the door except when Reba Jean had done it. She opened the door halfway and peered out; in slithered a very caring individual. He introduced himself as a consultant from the Care and Concern Committee who just wanted to make sure she was in a good frame of mind for the Easter Holiday and upcoming busyness that Reba Jean had in store.

Lady Jane was taken aback for a bit, but he oozed care and concern and attention. She thought it was a bit odd but brought him in to show him the library. He saw the bricked-off hallways and patted her on the back, assuring her that soon she would be able to walk the length of those. He spied the Crimson Vault but just rubbed her arm reassuringly. He was careful to not let any of his black ooze drip on her alerting her to his real identity.

Dripping with false pretense, he guided her to her armchair and knelt down next to her begging her to tell him all her troubles. He pulled out a quill and began to write down notes on a scroll he produced. He pretended to listen carefully, but inwardly he was struggling to keep up the pretense. Oh, how he just wanted to pounce on her and destroy every shred of self-imposed sanity that she thought she had.

The essence of the holy things in the library was making his skin burn, and he almost understood how humans felt when they were allergic to something. He was very careful to not touch or even go near the Ancient One or the second Golden Sword. He had a near miss when Lady Jane had trailed her fingers in the fountain of Living Water and had flicked them to dry them off.

Catching a glimpse of the archway leading to Sir Theo's library, he knew that would also be a strong, unsuspecting supporter of his effort. He listened to Lady Jane drone on and heard her mention Lady Constance. Oh! He knew who that was. Hmmm, that might be something to explore. If he could weave himself into Lady Constance's or Lady Matilda's influence on her then he was assured of victory.

Lady Jane was lulled into a sense of comfort by Insecurity's false persona. Oh, that creepy sinister interloper of days gone by had tried to make her like him, but this new visitor was much different, or so she thought. She felt like she had found another friend. Wait, he hadn't actually said his name, hmmm, oh well, she felt like she had known him forever. She would have company now when Reba Jean was having to deal with life.

Insecurity tried to think of a name that would be charming and disarming to call himself. He hadn't thought this far ahead; in fact, he half expected not to be able to gain direct access to the library at all. A bit surprised at Lady Jane's gullibility, he, nevertheless, used it to his advantage. He sent word to his band of followers to keep weaving their attacks on the outside while he worked his wiles on the inside.

Reba Jean was not fully aware that Insecurity had actually made it inside the library. There was an odd anxious knot in her stomach, but she dismissed it as hunger. She had to cut back on what she ate; she had gained so much of her weight back in just one week. It was really discouraging to see all her hard work and her working hard had had the opposite effect on her weight. It was probably stress with all that was going on in her life. She had looked through pictures this morning from years past and had noticed even eight years ago she had had skin blemishes for Easter pictures. She found that disconcerting but realized that some things obviously never changed.

Lady Jane stopped rambling to Insecurity and found herself nodding off to sleep. She rarely was able to sleep like Reba Jean did, but Insecurity had lulled her into a false sense of security. He said he would tend to the library if she wanted him to take care of it for a little bit. She just needed to close her eyes for just a few minutes.

Insecurity waited for Lady Jane to follow his "caring" suggestion and chortled to himself when she did exactly that. He then began to silently wander the aisles looking for any books that he could use to help his agenda.

Reba Jean started to get a strong headache. She had felt it earlier and had taken her headache medicine; now it seemed to be happening again, and she couldn't take more medicine. Not realizing that it was mental and not physical, she rubbed her temples and tried to type more in her book. She was really trying to have it done on time to give to the publisher in May. Headaches this strong were pretty rare, and she felt fatigue set in upon her. Getting up to get a glass of water, she wondered if she was forgetting to do something. At her age, if she didn't write things down, she wouldn't always remember to do them.

Her eyes got blurry as she sat back down to look at the screen. Her book might need to be set aside; she had been staring at the screen too long again. Rubbing the blemish on her chin, she winced and hoped it would be healed in the next two days. No wonder people thought she didn't look as old as she was with acne sprouting out on her face. That might

145

explain why no one really seemed to take her seriously when she actually had a head on her shoulders. Well, she was used to people not thinking she was of any worth to them.

Fighting waves of that old enemy of insecurity and the need for validation and self-worth, she decided to save her added chapters and rest for a few minutes on the couch before it was time for supper. She didn't understand why she was so sleepy, but that too was part of her normal life. She laughed at the thought of "normal" and then realized that most people with crazy minds were the normal ones; the empty-headed people were the ones that truly weren't normal. At least that is what she tried to tell herself as she closed her eyes.

Insecurity could hear these thoughts as he stood in the library. He loved hearing his thoughts and words bounce around in this human cage. As he listened, he found a name he could call himself. Worth, yes, that is what he decided to tell Lady Jane his name was. She would never need to know that her new friend was really her enemy.

Mr. Insidious was so proud of himself for choosing Insecurity to be his surrogate. His strategy and prowess were becoming a success. He watched him gain access to the library and weave his ministrations around Lady Jane. Even Reba Jean conversely was affected by what was happening in the library. Lord Rabboni might have used the Overseer to banish him, but there were plenty more minions to bring Lady Jane and crazy Reba Jean to their knees, begging for relief.

Insecurity leaned back against a bookshelf, narrowing his eyes as he watched Lady Jane doze. He had about two more weeks before his mission was to be evaluated. He had plenty of time to weave his way into their lives. They would consider him their friend while he inwardly wreaked havoc on them mentally. Their mental state would affect all their other states, and then he would have the victory for the evil forces of the Dark Realm.

Reba Jean shivered violently. Was it the air conditioner she sat under, or was it something more? Still shivering, she decided to put on a sweater and some fuzzy warm socks. A little thought niggled at the back of her mind, not sure if she should explore that or ignore it. Walking down the hallway, she tried to discern what it was. The elusive thought seemed just out of her grasp, her headache was dissipating with the water, and she knew her husband would be home soon.

Wondering if it was something she should pray about or let go of, she stood there undecided and still shivering. The sweater was itchy, and she was still shivering. "Help me, Lord," she breathed a prayer almost defiantly just in case this was something she needed to pray about. Still shivering, she felt like something was warning her to pay attention.

The warm socks helped, but the sweater was still itchy. She made a cup of coffee as her husband drove in the driveway. She had a knot of anxiety still in her stomach. Something was up, but she had no time to deal with it now. Getting her husband settled and caught up on any news was the priority. He settled down to wind down from work, and she had a few moments to think again about what the problem could be.

Sipping her coffee, she cast around in her head for any issues. Her husband had made a face when she hadn't gotten a gift for the party tomorrow. She really had no clue what to buy; she had some items to re-gift, but he did not seem overly thrilled with that suggestion.

She read a lot into his body language as he often tried not to say anything that would bring a confrontation. He had a real way of making her unsure of herself, rarely happy or content with how she did things. It was nearly thirty years of this; sometimes, she wondered how they had made it this long together.

The coffee tried to calm her nerves while the sweater made her skin crawl. What an odd juxtaposition. An itchy calm? Closing her eyes again, she listened to the hymns still playing on the sound system. They were soothing to her mind, and she wondered if she had imagined that little niggle of alarm. Lulled into a sense of peace, she tried to shrug off the odd little feeling.

"Oh, this coffee is sooo good," she thought to herself. The sweater, however, was about to drive her crazy. The air conditioner was off; the coffee was warm; it was time to shed this itchy, hairy thing. That odd feeling in her stomach was hopefully hunger, although she did not really feel like eating. Feeling restless with the idea that something might be wrong, she paced around the room and decided to turn on the tv in hopes she could find something worth watching.

Lady Jane ignored any faint sounds from inside and outside the library; she hadn't had any real rest in years. Whether she was really asleep or not was hard to tell, but she sure was soaking in the moment of inactivity on her part. She brushed off the thought that she needed to be vigilant. The Overseer had banished Mr. Insidious and his crew; peace had been given, so surely there was nothing to watch out for now.

The two women had an underlying sense that something wasn't quite right, but it wasn't strong enough to put them on full alert. Insecurity made sure they weren't overly alarmed at his presence. He hadn't been actually introduced to Reba Jean; he still contemplated if he could deceive her. It probably would depend on her interactions with Lord Rabboni. He would need to make sure the Overseer wasn't in control when he was introduced. The Overseer would know immediately who he was, and he too would be banished.

Reba Jean decided she was probably just hungry and needed to eat something while she channel surfed. Her husband wanted a late supper, and he was zoned out in his office playing his game on the computer. Any thoughts of spiritual warfare seemed to be lulled into a false sense of security. Things weren't right, but neither did they seem to be all wrong. It was that in-between state that should have bothered her more.

Exhaling, she tried to shrug off the unnamed feeling of worry and anxiety that was forming in the pit of her stomach. Whatever was going on, it would probably manifest itself soon enough. It was easier to deal with a named dread than an un-named one, she reasoned to herself. She needed to escape into some semblance of mindlessness and turn off the crazy trains that threatened to derail in her mind again.

Insecurity found that he could leave the door just slightly ajar to the library, and the chime wouldn't sound. He carefully inched it open and let in Anxiety and Worry into the library. Anxiety had been here in the past, and Worry was a bit scared of his own shadow, but with good reason. They slipped in and hid in the back corners of the library out of sight. Just having them here made Insecurity feel even stronger and more capable of handling this mission.

Lady Jane felt a few cold drafts but did not want to wake up from her half-sleep. She felt goosebumps rise on her arms but just snuggled down into her chair and curled up into a ball of lethargy. Her new friend said he would watch the library for her. It was about time someone came to help her share the burden of responsibility. Reba Jean helped sometimes, but she didn't live in the library every minute of every hour like she did.

Mr. Insidious rubbed his claw-like hands together as he saw his minions enter silently into place in the library of secrets. They were on a secret mission, and their presence was still a secret. Oh, how he loved secrets. Secrets could do real damage to any human. He couldn't wait to see how this all played out in the next couple of weeks. The catalyst would be the Women's Conference, but that didn't mean he couldn't have his victory before then.

The next morning, Reba Jean felt a little paranoid as she researched how many pages and words a novel should have. She was worried that she would only have what amounted to a short story, and somehow, that seemed inadequate. However, she may not have two hundred pages, but she obviously was going to have enough words. She could hear her husband's frequent comments and critiques in her head about run-on sentences and too many descriptive words. She was trying to paint a word picture; some scenes required various descriptive words. Fighting down the feeling of insecurity, she tried to remember that God had given her this story, and He would do as He liked with it.

Insecurity rubbed his hands together in anticipation; he had watched Reba Jean's dreams during the night. He felt her anxious emotions this morning as she fretted over her book. He glanced towards Lady Jane to find her awake and watching him with a puzzled expression on her face.

"You don't sleep either?" she inquired of him.

"I am just like you, my dear, only an avatar; I am not mortal," he replied laconically. Lady Jane actually liked this answer, and she felt even more comfortable with this new friend. He had assuaged her doubts and fears with his casual, relaxed demeanor. She glanced around the library and saw an odd shoe dangling in mid-air and some books helter-skelter, but nothing too alarming to set her on the defensive.

It was going to be a busy day today, and Reba Jean just wanted to crawl away and hide. It should be a day of rest, yet it seemed that every time she needed rest, all she ended up with was a full-to-overflowing schedule. If she wasn't careful, she would grumble away every essence of peace she had felt yesterday.

She gave herself a stern talking to and tried to focus her thoughts on her devotions for the day. Any time her husband was home, he was a huge distraction. He expected her to come to his every beck and call regardless of what she was in the middle of doing or not doing. His agenda was always paramount, and many times this made her feel more like an employee and less like a helpmeet.

She was starting to feel crankier than even just a few minutes ago; this would not bode well for a day that should be fun. She knew something was going out of balance, probably due to adequate sleep. She had had only one disturbing scene in one of her dreams, and she had shut that down really quickly. The rest of the dreams were really odd for her mind to be struggling with. She could blame social media for her mind's inability to process certain situations. If she thought it, she would dream about it, sure as the world.

Lady Jane puzzled over her ability to have fallen asleep. That had not happened without anesthesia before. Was this something to be concerned about, or was this part of the aging process of the human body she was dwelling in? She winced at how that statement sounded, as if she was a demon possessing someone. Then, her thought stuttered to a stop, and there was a stillness both in her thoughts and in Reba Jean's. It was disconcerting; did Lady Jane have her own thoughts?

With a sudden swing in Insecurity's direction, she remembered he had not introduced himself yesterday. Pinning him with her huge dark eyes, she enquired of his lineage. Soothingly, he introduced himself as Worth, from the Curtis family originating from the Deep South. He apologized for not having remembered his manners; he had just been so enamored of her. Again, his soothing tone and relaxed manner fell upon her like a security blanket.

Something was still buzzing around in the back of Reba Jean's head as she tried to calm her emotions and qualms about the day. She had a feeling she needed a good long time of prayer, and sadly, she doubted that would happen today. There still seemed to be something amiss; she just couldn't put her finger on it. Syncing communication with her husband to make sure they were both on the same page for the day, she tried to will away the anxious feeling in her stomach.

Opening her devotions to 2 Kings, she forced herself to focus on what she could glean from God's Word this morning. This feeling of coming unraveled was increasing; it was going to need some intervention of the Heavenly sort.

Chapter 14

As it seemed to be the situation lately, it was days before more of the book was to be written or even the library to be visited. A few more scenarios had come to mind, and yet a sense of hurried restlessness frustrated the writing process. It was more like trying to get the book finished was more important than fleshing out the scenes. This was somewhat aggravating yet intriguing. There was also that lingering desire to just ruthlessly edit the whole book. The research about writing a first novel was a bit discouraging, yet there was the reminder that God had given this book. This reminder always came to the forefront any time insecurities arose pertaining to it.

Reba Jean sat down to mentally inventory the last few days; she thought of some changes that needed to be implemented in the library. The ability to change or transform it had come to her just a day ago, and she was anticipating the thought of how to transform the library into a place that the Lord Himself would be comfortable visiting.

Wasting no more time, she ran up the stairs and opened the library door. It had an odd little catch to it as she opened it. This caught her attention; she inspected the door, the frame, and then the latch. The frame looked a bit warped, and the door seemed a fraction larger than it used to. The latch, however, seemed to have some sort of gadget on it that had not been there previously. The hair on the back of her neck stiffened for a fraction of a second. Entering the library, she noticed that although the sun was shining in the windows, there was an odd tension in the air. The undercurrent made her feel insecure yet again. Breathing a prayer, she moved along through the atrium to the inner aisles.

Lady Jane heard the door latch as it caught on the special latch that Worth had installed the other day. He had needed some fresh air, he said. The atmosphere in the library was making him sick, and it was stifling. He told her that instead of always interrupting her by knocking when he wanted in, he would just put his own latch on the door. She had almost thought he would never return, but there he was. Some days he was strong and engaging; other days, he seemed so sickly and needed her every attention. Her new friend was an enigma to her, and yet she was very defensive of him.

She had had a short visit with Lady Matilda, which had felt more like gossip, and she knew that Reba Jean wouldn't like that. Lady Constance had sent her love, but oddly this didn't encourage her as it usually did. She was just so enamored by Worth and his ability to just be so charming and chatty. He asked a lot of questions and gave her a different perspective on things.

Reba Jean came upon Lady Jane as she contemplated all these things. Reba Jean looked around and wondered at the feeling that had grown stronger in this room. Spying a shadow lurking in the corner, she frowned. Spinning back towards Lady Jane, she raised an eyebrow at her petulant expression. A bit taken aback by the wild look in Lady Jane's eyes, she paused before she said anything.

The two women stared at each other without speaking for a few more moments. Worth did not like Reba Jean. She smelled of the Holy One, and she would need to be dealt with carefully. Easter had been really rough on him being in this library. He had managed to secure the door as he left so that he could return at will. He had had to leave many times; whenever Reba Jean got close to the Holy One, his strength would leave him. He did not like being sick, but other times he was able to push through, and his purpose was resolved.

Reba Jean stood really still, watching the shadow carefully. It definitely belonged to something, not from any of the furnishings or the misty tendrils. She felt a shiver start along her backbone, and she knew it was time to bring this shadow out into the light. "Lady Jane, darling, do you have a visitor?" she tried to ask casually.

Lady Jane, somewhat defensive but with a growing boldness, decided to introduce Worth as he had titled himself. Drawing him out of the shadows, she boldly introduced Worth to Reba Jean. Babbling about his intelligence and wonderful perspective, she found herself acting like a schoolgirl in love. Worth came out into the light and affected a very debonair attitude with Reba Jean. He had to charm her into letting him keep access to the library. What he did not realize is that when he ran out of the library on Easter Sunday night, Reba Jean had been at the altar praying for the Lord to deal with her insecurities about everything. He only knew he had not been able to stay; he just had to get out of there.

Worth bowed low over Reba Jean's hand in an old-time manner of a gentleman. He spoke low soothing words as he introduced himself as Worth of the family Curtis from the Deep South. Lady Jane watched him and smiled; yes, he was his old strong self again today. She felt a tinge of jealousy over his attention to Reba Jean but tried not to let it show. She wanted all his attention; not even Reba Jean was aware of how much she needed a friend in the library with her at all times.

Reba Jean glanced over to the Ancient One and remembered the recent events and her purpose for needing the library transformed. Worth tried to draw her attention away from the Ancient One and began to weave his charming questions around her. Reba Jean, however, began to feel like a spider was crawling on her. She shuddered and couldn't shake the feeling of the creepy crawlies.

Worth realized that he wasn't making as much progress with Reba Jean as he had hoped, so he turned his attention back to Lady Jane. She preened under his attentive charming ways. They linked arms and strolled down the aisles of bookshelves, chattering about the books contained there. Reba Jean inhaled slowly and felt like she could catch a breath as they created distance between themselves.

Eyes slanting thoughtfully, Reba Jean took this moment to carefully pick up the Ancient One from its long-time position on the old, rugged table. She closed her eyes and imagined a beautiful golden-hued marble podium. Opening her eyes, there it was in all its radiant splendor. Placing the Ancient One on the new podium, she carefully moved the old, rugged table in front of the locked door of the Crimson Vault. Looking around for the golden gossamer from weeks before, she couldn't find it.

Calling out to Lady Jane to help her search, she was alarmed to learn that Worth had turned the gossamer into a dragonfly. Lady Jane had thought this was amazing when he had done it a few days ago. Now, when she saw Reba Jean's face, it did not seem so harmless. Worth tried to calm the Mistress of the house down and offered to change it back if he could find where it had flitted off to. He needed to act as self-deprecating as possible, or he knew he would be evicted permanently like his predecessors had been.

Reba Jean started a mental list of all the weird things in the library that would need rectifying today. She had learned that it was not good to let these things go unchecked. This Worth character would need to be removed, and the knowledge of that and his spell over Lady Jane felt a bit daunting. First, she needed to finish transforming the library to its new specifications. She drew down a misty tendril to form a quill and began to write in a book she had pulled from a locked chest.

Worth couldn't resist sidling closer to see what secrets she had kept under lock and key. He had heard the story of the key to the vault, but he had not seen her use a key on the chest. These secrets had not been on display before to his knowledge. He slid in closer and leaned over her shoulder. In dark foreboding ink, she was writing down temptations that she had endured over the weekend. His eyes widened as he tried to read them all without her knowing it. This could be great information to use and forward on to his captains.

Reba Jean knew Worth was trying to see, but she was writing in code. She did not want anyone to know these secrets. They had nearly been the death of her. They were not new temptations but recurring ones. It was getting almost laughable when they would attack her with their fiery darts. She had realized a few years ago that if it went against God's Word, then it was a temptation, and she did NOT have to give into it, no matter how terrifyingly strong they were. She well understood the power they had over her, yet she continued to resist as the Word of God commanded her to do.

Worth could not understand anything she was writing; it looked like an ancient language. He silently motioned for Lady Jane to come and have a look. She peered timidly over Reba Jean's shoulder, and she was able to understand what was being written. Her eyes grew large and fearful when she realized how close to death they had been in the last few days. If Reba Jean had given in to those attacks, neither of them would be here today! Lady Jane raised her eyes back to Worth, but this time he did not look as harmless as before. In spite of his friendliness, she began to inwardly question his perspective these last few days.

Reba Jean put down the quill, closed the book, and it locked automatically. She placed it back in the chest, and that too locked automatically. Worth was taken aback by the security features that were in place in the library. He then giggled to himself at the thought that the library entrance did not seem to have any special security to protect it. The two women looked at each other, then turned around to look at Worth. He squirmed a bit under their gaze and then tried to be as debonair as he could. The mistress and her mental avatar, however, seemed to be having a wordless conversation. He could not read their thoughts. This would never do; he must reassert his control. Reba Jean needed to leave so that he could better manipulate Lady Jane. His special latch would need to be recalibrated to lock Reba Jean OUT of the library.

Reba Jean mentally asked Lady Jane if the Overseer had approved Worth's presence in the library. She reminded her that just because someone knocked on the library door did not mean they had to be let in. Lady Jane hung her head silently as she realized that anyone that had to knock on the library door probably wasn't meant to have access. Then she stubbornly telegraphed back that Reba Jean herself had knocked before. Then, she hung her head again; that silent question about the Overseer had struck a chord deep inside of her.

Worth spied the beginning transformative changes taking place and Lady Jane's head hanging in dejection. He started to think that maybe he needed reinforcements. No longer did he puff up with pride thinking he was better than Doubtful or Anxiety or even Mr. Insidious. He started getting all creepy crawly himself, then he noticed the golden dust motes were falling like glitter on him.

Those things were like little, tiny sparks shocking and burning him! He started dancing and slapping them away. The two women noticed his discomfort and soon realized the cause of his crazy-looking jig. Reba Jean tried not to laugh, but she did snicker once. Then, she bowed her head, kneeled by the golden podium, and prayed. Lady Jane held her breath as she sensed the arrival of the Overseer into the library.

Worth panicked; he felt like a thousand mosquitos had homed in on him. He began to feel sick and weak as he had previously at various times. An overpowering holy presence filled the library; the Overseer had arrived. Worth fell to his knees, retching and squirming in agony. With a sprinkle of living water from the fountain, Lady Jane tried to revive him. This, however, had the opposite effect on Worth; it washed off his pretense and exposed him for exactly who and what he was! Insecurity was on full display; his lineage and pedigree were of the basest sort. Lady Jane was appalled at how easily she had been duped!

With the last ounce of remaining strength, worthless Insecurity crawled to the door and rolled out into the underworld. Reba Jean and the Overseer went to the library's door, removed the offending latch mechanism, and the Overseer touched the door of the library, transforming it into a very securely guarded portal.

Spying the dragonfly as it crashed to the floor, it transformed back into shimmering gossamer as Insecurity's control of it ceased. Placing the gossamer on the old, rugged table, Reba Jean then proceeded to put a beautiful old oil lamp in the center of the table using the gossamer as a table runner. With the help of the golden dust motes, she wrote a Scripture from the Ancient One onto the table. "Thy word is a lamp unto my feet, and a light unto my path."

Lady Jane bowed to her face and waited for her chastisement from the Overseer. Instead, He turned and looked at Reba Jean; He held HER accountable for Lady Jane's actions. Reba Jean understood clearly that although her mind wasn't saved, she needed to stop letting it have control of her thoughts. Seeking forgiveness, she knelt and prayed for a long time. The Overseer wafted her prayer up to the Holy One of Heaven.

Satisfied that things were once again under the approval of King Abba and Lord Rabboni, the Overseer went back down to the living room where He usually resided. The two women sat still for a while, then began re-organizing and transforming the library. It felt so peaceful and serene without Insecurity whispering suppositions and different perspectives around them. He had woven such a false sense of security that they did not realize it was really insecurity at the core.

A soft sound overhead drew their eyes upward; gently swaying in the breeze was that odd shoe that had appeared last week. Reba Jean snapped her fingers at it, and it vanished. She no longer felt like she was waiting for the other shoe to drop, so to speak. Dusting her hands off as if they were dirty, she looked around for anything else that might need changing or transforming.

Lady Jane felt stronger the more changes that were made. It wasn't a pride-filled strength but more like a very strong state of mind. Without Insecurity holding her attention all the time, she could see things so clearly. She would need to find a way not to be so easily duped by visitors from the Dark Realm. She noticed how each time there was a battle, a new artifact or spiritual symbol was installed. Why wasn't just having the Ancient One enough for her to rely on?

Reba Jean watched Lady Jane for a few minutes, and she motioned to the misty tendrils for help. They formed themselves into a blanket and picnic basket, letting the two women have a lovely imaginary lunch. Lady Jane giggled when she stated, "This is food for thought." It was a nice repast after such a busy month with such an upheaval that seemed to happen way too often.

With a sudden leap to her feet, Reba Jean wandered off and walked down one of those walled-off hallways. She touched the walled-off area, and it opened under her touch. Inside the empty alcove, she formed a room full of all sorts of strange characters and scenarios. Lady Jane peered into the room and immediately recognized the scenes enfolding! It was now a room holding all of Reba Jean's dreams whilst she was asleep. "Ok, my dear, I know the burden this has been upon you and has worn you slap out," explained Reba Jean. "I need to be the one that monitors my thoughts and subsequent dreams, not you. Let's try keeping all my weird dreams in this room; keep the door closed so they can't escape into the rest of the library. Every day I will be the one that evaluates the dreams so that any action can be taken immediately. You are now absolved of any responsibility for monitoring my dreams."

Lady Jane stood stock still; this had never happened before. She had thought that she would be forever awake every night watching bizarre scenes unfold and have to awaken Reba Jean when they became too intense. With a puzzled expression, she looked at Reba Jean; what was to become of her? Reba Jean read Lady Jane's thoughts and assured her that the library was still her home, just not her job to be in charge of any longer.

This was a whole new chapter in Lady Jane's life; she could just sit and enjoy the library. Was Reba Jean really up to the task of keeping everything under control and up to the standards that King Abba had instituted and declared?

Lady Jane felt a sudden fear descend on her. The Women's Conference was coming up next weekend; would Reba Jean survive? Lady Jane looked around at the new security measures and the new door on the library. Maybe all these things would help ensure the library's integrity and strength. No more critters allowed in this transformed place.

Chapter 15

Insecurity tumbled into the dark realm, still feeling the shocking tingles of the golden dust motes. He shook himself off and looked around to see if anyone had noticed his disgraceful return. Sure enough, there was a messenger from Mr. Insidious demanding his report in person. He stomped into Mr. Insidious' crusty cavern and stood there with his arms folded defiantly.

Mr. Insidious gave him a scathing visual inspection without uttering a word. He well knew that when Reba Jean was heeding the Word of the Holy One, she became very formidable with HIS power. He hoped that Insecurity had planted seeds that would bear fruit in the next few weeks. Reba Jean had installed a new security system, but she did not have control over the libraries represented around her. He did not chastise Insecurity; he just slapped him on the back of the head and sent him back into the fight to see how many of Reba Jean's inner circle he could manipulate and influence instead.

Insecurity rubbed the back of his head and climbed up into the human realm again. Who should he whisper to next? He found Gossip hovering, and his eyes gleamed. Oh yes, Gossip was still a strong ally and a huge proponent of the dark lord's long game. He and Gossip sat together and strategized over their next targets. Insecurity felt his self-worth increase, and he realized he was still a vital part of the destructive forces.

Reba Jean was still bothered by her conversation with a family member over the weekend. She wondered if what she had done in the exchanging of perspective, opinion, and information was considered gossip. She even went so far as to look up the meaning of gossip. Talking about anyone, even if just exchanging information, made her feel like she was gossiping. She also knew that she too often "exchanged information" about people with her husband. Part of the definition applied, yet the other part did not. This seemed like an oxymoron to her. She would need to figure this gossip issue out long before the Women's Conference arrived so that she would know how to interact with the other women.

Her boss was all excited about this Conference, but Reba Jean was still trying to decide if she had made the wrong decision after all.

She would be rooming with family members, and she really hoped that she could be quiet and discreet instead of trying to be the center of attention. Her dreams lately had been of every little thing she had thought of during the day and then some. That Dream Room in the library was a good way to monitor what was bothering her while she was asleep. She was very concerned that the Conference would have an ungodly influence on her. Determined not to let this happen, she began to pray even more earnestly for help to get some real spiritual food from this Conference.

Lady Jane saw Reba Jean in deep prayer; she looked around at the tendrils and the golden dust motes to see how they would react. With no immediate reaction, Lady Jane understood that these prayers were for future events, not current or past. Catching a glint, she saw the lovely crystal stone twinkling in the gently receding bricked-off hallway. Every day that wall seemed more transparent, and it seemed to be more of a hallway than a blocked-off area. Reba Jean had not even visited that wall or hallway today. She found that a bit odd but realized that Insecurity had taken most of the attention off of the other library happenings.

As Reba Jean prayed, the Ancient One seemed to grow much larger on its new beautiful podium. The oil lamp on the old, rugged table glowed brightly while the blue butterfly fluttered over an end of the gossamer. Lady Jane was in awe of how the library was being transformed right before her eyes. Reba Jean truly did need to be here more often, she surmised.

With a lifting of her head, Reba Jean reached up to another misty tendril and had it turn into a fountain pen. Pulling a book out of her skirt pocket, Reba Jean sat back on the blanket they had eaten on and began to write in her book. This was the best place to write her book, for this book was about this very library. Lady Jane sank down on the blanket gracefully and felt herself nod off into a daydream sort of sleep. It was such a different feeling than when she had been lulled into a pseudo-coma with Insecurity. This felt more like being at deep peace out in a meadow of buttercups and daisies. This was rest and peace from that gift that King Abba had given them.

Reba Jean wrote away, the pages soaking up her words as she tried to describe the library, Lady Jane, and the various issues that had to be dealt with in order to have a library of serenity. Time flew by on the wings of a butterfly as she became lost in the world of the library. She giggled when she realized this was very much like being "lost in thought." Her watch told her that not as much time had passed as it had seemed. Time was always different here in the library than in the outer world. Rubbing her face with her hands, she sat back on her heels and looked at her progress. She had almost one hundred pages of this chaotic saga, and it had taken her this long to get to this amount. Shaking off any qualms or insecurity as quickly as they tried to worm their way into her consciousness, she kept writing.

Jerking to attention, she realized truly she had been lost in thought, but this time no misty tendrils or chaos had presented themselves. This was good; it meant that the library was not reacting to every little nuance. It was good to have more control in keeping this place beautiful and serene. With a thought, she stood up and went back to the room of Dreams.

She checked the latch on the door and added more security features to make sure no one ever saw these dreams. Lady Jane would just have an honorary role from now on in this library.

A tapping sound started somewhere off in the endless caverns of the library. The women looked at each other bewildered. Together they set off to investigate the sound. Aisle after aisle, they walked down past Sir Theo's archway, past all the usual chests and artifacts that they were familiar with seeing. Following the sound that had not stopped, they finally found themselves in front of a closet, the door was locked, however. The tapping became more insistent and louder, but Reba Jean refused to open the door. She knew that whatever secrets were locked away in that closet needed to stay there. The Overseer had inspected every inch of this library; if it was locked up, then it needed to stay locked!

Lady Jane felt her arm held in a firm grip, and she saw that Reba Jean had decided that this was not a closet that needed to be opened no matter what. With a finger to her lips, she led Lady Jane back down the maze of hallways, completely ignoring the tapping. As they passed the Ancient One, Reba Jean flipped the pages to Psalm 40:1-4; the words rose up from the page in a golden strand of letters, and like an arrow, they flew straight down the hallway to that door. Emblazoning themselves on the outside of the door, the tapping sound ceased, and the library returned to its necessary balance.

Together they flipped through the Psalms reading more words of King Abba written down in the Ancient One. A few pages later they read Psalm 34:13-15, and Reba Jean gasped. This passage was exactly what she needed to hear concerning the upcoming Women's Conference. The whole intended theme of the conference should hinge on this passage. It would for her; she just needed to stick to it and not give in to lies, insecurity, gossip, or any other insidious mechanizations of the evil one.

Inhaling with a sense of purpose, she knew this passage was a direct answer to her earnest prayers for help. Walking back to her book, she closed it gently and put it back in her skirt. She hugged Lady Jane and encouraged her to stay close to the fountain or the Ancient One and to enjoy the new atmosphere in the transformed library.

Reba Jean softly latched the door of the library behind her and blinked a few times as she re-entered reality. So much had happened in such a short time, yet it had only happened inside of the library and in her own heart. Outwardly, the day and time just ticked by as usual. It was time to check the laundry and rest a few minutes before supper. There was mid-week prayer meeting tonight, and boy did she need to be there for that. She had missed too many of them for all sorts of supposedly valid reasons and some not very valid ones.

Tomorrow would probably bring forth another day of hard work; she did not want to complain, but she did miss days like today when she could be home. Was that lazy or selfish of her? Reba Jean pondered this dilemma. It was a good day thus far; she really did enjoy being at home and taking care of her house and husband. With that thought in mind, she had better get to it. The need to change out the laundry superseded her desire to flop on the chaise lounge and vegetate.

She had one hundred pages written in her book; it still needed editing, but this was a great accomplishment for her personally. She thanked the Lord for getting her this far. Again, she reminded herself that this book was from the Lord, and its future was in His capable hands.

As soon as she returned home from church, she ran up the stairs to the library. She couldn't wait to discuss tonight's message with Lady Jane. It had been exactly on target; she was still in awe every time God seemed to speak directly to her situation on a personal level. Opening the door, she breezed in through the atrium, humming a merry little tune. Lady Jane heard the joyful noise and came to investigate. Together they sat down in the atrium, and with the glow of the beautiful, old oil lamp, they discussed the sermon notes.

Malachi 3 had been the text concerning the remnant that was faithful to God, in spite of the world they lived in. The title of the message had been Characteristics of the Remnant, and the first point seemed obvious as it stated that their hearts were moved by the fear of God as stated in verse sixteen of that chapter.

The second point, however, was so pertinent to their current situation. It stated that their minds were filled with the thoughts of God. Reba Jean expounded on this point further from her notes. She instructed Lady Jane that their minds needed to be so focused on God that there was not any room for anything or anyone else. Then she stated that the third point that was so very helpful to her with the gossip issue. The third point of tonight's message had been that a characteristic of the remnant that was faithful was that their tongues were busy with things of God. Wow, that was just so relevant to her fears about gossip and discord.

Her preacher had also made mention of a verse in Zephaniah 3 that she couldn't wait to look up and refresh her memory. It spoke of the Lord singing over His remnant. Oh, how she wanted to be there when the Lord began to sing with His people. "Can you even imagine this, Lady Jane?" she breathed in an awe-filled whisper. There was another point to the night's message, but the middle two made such an impact that she spent some time meditating on them. Lady Jane loved

168

it when Reba Jean spent time with her and their focus was on King Abba or Lord Rabboni.

What a great way to end a very event-filled day for the library and its curators. Reba Jean glanced down at her Bible that she had brought up with her to the library; her eyes fell on the words in Haggai 1, "Consider your way," and again, further down in a few more verses, it repeated, "Consider your ways." Pondering this further, she knew it was going to be up to her to apply this message and be no purveyor of gossip or backbiting. Instead of being so concerned about getting caught in it, she needed to be so focused on the Lord that He would be all that she could talk about.

Resolved to implement this from this moment and not wait until the ride to the conference, she silently commanded herself to be vigilant in this matter.

It was nearing time for bed, and she needed to pray about having calm, clean, peace-filled dreams. She hugged Lady Jane and told her to get some rest for tomorrow they were sure to be put to the test on this new resolution. It was gearing up to be another physically exhausting day; they would need to be rested so that their attitudes and moods were pleasing to God.

Lady Jane was still a bit unsure of this whole resting thing; she was so used to watching the dreams and being alert to any hint of trouble. Reba Jean assured her that it was no longer her responsibility. The Dream Room would record the dreams, and Reba Jean would evaluate what changes would need to be made during the daytime hours to change her future dreams.

Reaching up to snag a misty tendril, she began weaving a few of them together and soon had a soft cashmere blanket that she draped around Lady Jane and thus bid her a good night and sweet dreams of her own. Lady Jane watched Reba Jean glide out of the library as if on a golden cloud. She snuggled down with her new blanket and gazed dreamily at the light from the oil lamp. Listening, she could hear humming from Sir Theo's library, and the peace in the library lulled her to sleep.

Reba Jean still felt a bit restless; she knew she needed to go to bed, but she really needed to find something to calm the sudden flutter in her chest. Was this physical or spiritual, she wondered to herself. She gently laid her Bible down on the kitchen table and sat thoughtfully as she took inventory of her symptoms. She had so many various physical oddities lately that it was hard to know if anything was serious or just "normal" for her.

Knowing that she was going to be exhausted tomorrow, she decided to just try to head to bed and ask the Lord to settle her mind and body. She needed to ask Him also for more strength as she was still struggling with the effect her job had on her physically. Closing her eyes and rubbing her face, she sighed and still couldn't seem to settle her mind and body enough to go to sleep.

Against her better judgment, she decided to scroll through social media. Maybe there would be some inspiration or encouragement, or it would bore her enough to go to sleep. Mindless scrolling surely was not the proper treatment for whatever it was that ailed her. She was already impatient with herself at the very thought of doing it. It was no different than channel surfing the tv, unable to watch anything because all of it was ungodly and unfit for the faithful remnant.

She remembered her resolve and changed her mind. She would NOT scroll through social media like some sort of junkie. It was bedtime, and that is where she needed to be, not looking at what amounted to drivel at times. With firm resolve, she went to bid her husband goodnight and make herself crawl into bed. The feeling she had in the library already seemed to be going away, and that, too, bothered her. She hoped it had at least helped Lady Jane; the two of them needed to work together, not against each other.

Reba Jean paused for a minute, trying to recapture that moment she had while meditating on God's Word. Closing her eyes and focusing on the Lord, she felt a tingle in her stomach, and her head started aching. She had a sneaky suspicion that this might be the start of a spiritual attack. It was inevitable since she had resolved to be more spiritually minded. She almost giggled in spite of the seriousness of it.

Grabbing a banana on her way through the kitchen to the bedroom, she thought she would eat a banana just in case it was purely physical. Then she would pray herself to sleep, she hoped.

The lure of the social media siren seemed to beckon her as she passed the doorway of her husband's office next to the bedroom. She couldn't resist no matter her good intentions. She scrolled a little bit, but it just was not the panacea either for what ailed her. Instead, she got absorbed in a digital jigsaw puzzle. She liked the mystery ones; too many times she could not tell what the whole picture was until she had it finished. It was very challenging, yet relaxing, as it focused her mind solely on finding the pieces to fit together.

She remonstrated herself for her seeming addiction to scrolling or puzzles. Why wasn't just praying herself to sleep the right remedy? It would be days before she understood what was really going on in her life. Reba Jean would end up at yet another emotional or mental breaking point before she began to realize that this was the enemy's preparation work to destabilize her before the Women's Conference that was swiftly approaching.

Reba Jean sneaked up the stairs to the library quietly, already anticipating that it would be a fine mess after this weekend. She had made the mess, she was aware of this, and she would need to clean it up. What sort of mess would she find in this library of secrets? Opening the door carefully, she tried to adjust her eyes to the dark interior. The very faint glow from the oil lamp was barely a blur in the dense air that hovered all through the library.

Finding Lady Jane was going to be a problem from the get-go, that was definitely for sure. She had probably found something to hide under with all that had transpired since Reba Jean's last visit up here. Sticking her hands out in front of her, she started pushing her way through the dense, tangible air. Were these misty tendrils or something more? So difficult to discern, but knowing the resentment and frustration and all the myriad host of issues and emotional thoughts that had happened over the weekend, this she perceived was most likely a dark, foreboding fog.

She was lost in her own library without knowing where to turn or even how to find the Ancient One or the Golden Sword to cut through this mess. In the real world, she could just mutter to herself and think awful things, but here in the library is where they were stored and came to life. Pushing through the heavy air permeated with resentment and unthankfulness, she found herself finally in front of the oil lamp. Its wick was nearly burned down, and there seemed but a few drops of oil left! What if King Abba or Lord Rabboni came to gather her and Lady Jane Home?!!! What would they find?

Panicking, she dropped to her knees and cried out for mercy and forgiveness. Some of the air cleared around her, just enough to see shelves toppled over and locked chests wide open. No wonder it was so heavy in here; all those secrets that had been locked away had been let free once more to darken the very walls of the library with their horrific details. Was Lady Jane even in one piece?

Sobbing in horror, she sank to the floor and felt all sorts of unseen objects poking at her and pricking her skin. For every victory, every mountain, there seemed to be an immediate valley of darkness and terror to follow. Even if the dark lord of the evil realm from the nether world or his multitude of minions had been banished over and over again from the library, her very own feelings and secrets would nigh do her in for good.

Crying endless tears of misery and frustration, she became completely exhausted. The library was a very visual representation of all that she had felt and gone through in the last few days. It was honestly a very ugly picture of how she had succumbed to her exhaustion and how easy it was to cause a real blow to her relationship with God and everyone around her. She sank face first onto the floor, feeling the weight of all she had brought into the library.

Peering through the dark, musty, dank air, she tried to find a way to get to the Ancient One. Where was help when she needed it? In despair and feeling shame and defeat, Reba Jean uttered a wordless silent plea for help. She had done this, she berated herself. She had felt so victorious over Mr. Insidious and Insecurity and the countless other often unnamed minions that had attacked the library, yet its greatest enemy was HER! Wallowing in defeat and despair, the air just seemed to get heavier and darker. She couldn't hear anything except the voices of all the secrets and the wayward thoughts that were running rampant around the library. She heard more shelves crash over, causing her to curl into a fetal position.

Who would rescue her from herself?

Chapter 16

Mr. Insidious, along with Insecurity and his squad, watched in fascinating glee when they saw the effects of their influence on the people and situations surrounding Reba Jean in the last week. They did not need to actually get into her library; she was obviously a wreck waiting to happen! It just needed the right ingredients and the correct amount of pressure, and SNAP! There she falls apart, and they hadn't actually touched her.

Dancing around arm in arm, they stirred up resentment, disappointment, and exhaustion whipping them into a fine frenzy. It was definitely important to remember that lack of sleep and too much stress were the keys to defeating Reba Jean, turning her into a weapon of personal mass destruction.

If they did not overdo it and cause her to call out to the Lord of the Heavenly Realm, then they would definitely have utter and complete victory through this Women's Conference. Laughing wildly, they manipulated Reba Jean and her inner circle and threw in a puppy for good measure. Oh, that puppy, that was the total undoing of little Miss Goody-Two-Shoes! Where was her Sword and suit of armor for this?

The dark lord of the nether world would hear of this, not because Reba Jean was anything, but because now they had another key to the overall campaign. Throughout ages, exhaustion had forced a good many powerful spiritual leaders into a spiraling downspin. Mortal bodies were so frail that it often did not take much to cause great harm to them, just a sickness, circumstance, or stress, and they would forget who and Whose they were.

Reba Jean sobbed, but as she sobbed, she prayed. The more she prayed, the stronger she felt, and the heaviness over her spirit lightened. She was still tired, but she would catch up on her sleep here and there. It would be a difficult week with too many expectations from people around her that she would need to handle with care. As the air was beginning to be breathable again, she felt a confident resolve fill her being.

Pushing herself into a sitting position, she was struck by that word "confidant." In Spanish, the word "con" meant "with," and "fidant" sounded like "fidelis, or fidelity" which, of course, meant faithful, loyal, and able to put your trust in. A "confidante" was a French term for someone whom you could trust with your secrets. Her eyes grew large when she drew this comparison to her current situation in the library. She had opened locked secrets and had resorted to old ways of incorrectly handling pressure and stress instead of confiding in the very One Who was her Confidante. He could be trusted to carry her secrets; she didn't need to lock them away into chests and hope they never got free to cause damage.

A burst of resolve propelled Reba Jean straight in the direction of the Ancient One. Tripping over piles of debris and swatting away dark, misty tendrils, she pushed onward until she collapsed in front of the marble altar holding the Ancient One. With her last ounce of fortitude, she grabbed the hilt of the Golden Sword and held onto it with all her strength.

Now what? How would she collect all these secret feelings and emotions and mental mayhem, and then what would she do with them? The locked chests obviously weren't secure from her own traitorous tendencies. She began swinging the Golden Sword in swooping arcs waiting for some sort of revelation to come to her about what to do. Twirling around with the Golden Sword, she saw it was slicing through the misty tendrils and changing the secrets that it touched. Fascinated, she continued to swing away at the emotions and mental images of frustration and resentment that were clouding the atmosphere in the library.

What were the secrets being changed into? She blinked in disbelief; why, they were being changed into those tiny golden dust motes that often transformed things in the library into beautiful symbols from the Holy One? This was how her mental transformation was taking place. She watched closely, and every time the Golden Sword touched a secret or gloomy emotion there was a sizzle, and it was turned to ash. Then the ash was transformed into the beautiful, golden dust motes. She heard the pages of the Ancient One flip in rapid succession as if in answer to her mental questions. It was highlighting in beautiful golden script the words of Isaiah 61:3 "To appoint unto them that mourn in Zion, to give unto them beauty for ashes, the oil of joy for mourning, the garment of praise for the spirit of heaviness; that they might be called trees of righteousness, the planting of the LORD, that He might be glorified."

What would this do to Lady Jane, wherever she was? Oh, she hoped she found her before it was too late. Things in the library were so much more visual than in Reba Jean's usual world of so-called reality. Still swinging the Golden Sword, she cleared away all the mayhem and clutter. It was hard work to fix the chaos that she herself had created in this place that should be a sanctuary, not a cesspool.

Lifting the final bookshelf back into its upright position, she spied Lady Jane lying crumpled and broken under the weight of the bookshelf after it had fallen over on top of her. With a heartbroken sob, she gently checked Lady Jane to see if she was still alive. Just the slightest breath was in her still, and Reba Jean carried her to the Ancient One upon its beautiful marble pedestal. It looked so much like an altar that she often thought of it as such. Laying Lady Jane gently down at the base of the altar, she began praying for her. "Please, oh my Father, turn my mess into something that You can use for Your glory."

Reba Jean prayed humbly and earnestly for Lady Jane's restoration or else her transformation.

Lady Jane could hear a murmured prayer near her face; she hurt all over, and she felt completely shattered inside. When the battle in the library had started, she was shocked to realize that it was Reba Jean who was doing the damage without any help from the Evil Realm. The escaped secrets had chased and tortured her, voices had tormented her, she couldn't seem to escape; then she had tripped, and as she fell, she took a bookshelf down with her. She was pinned and losing all will to even live. With the last little energy she had, she put herself into self-preservation mode. This shut her brain down (if that was possible), like a mental coma. The damage to her body however was unsightly.

Reba Jean continued to pray for Lady Jane and her library; it was vital that restoration and healing were to take place. She felt a feather-like touch on her and looked up to see a golden tendril from the Ancient One alerting her to a Presence. The Overseer had once again arrived to answer the call for help. He knelt over Lady Jane and anointed her with oil and a special balm from Gilead. He looked piercingly at Reba Jean, who bowed her head in submission and surrender. She heard His Voice within her tell her that He would help Lady Jane, but she would be forever scarred and marred by Reba Jean's actions. It would be a visible reminder of what happens when she did not control her thoughts.

His Presence flowed through the library, refilling the oil lamp, and taking all the broken chests and turning them into a large wooden barrel such as was seen in ancient times. This He filled with oil to keep the lamp always burning bright until King Abba would send Lord Rabboni for her Homegoing. With tears of humble thankfulness, Reba Jean felt His Presence leave the library. Lady Jane sat up, she was no longer the beauty that she had been, but there was a very special glow about her from being touched by the Overseer's healing ministrations.

Reba Jean did not know what to say to Lady Jane. How could she even forgive her for nearly killing her? Lady Jane saw the sorrow-filled expression and the humility. Part of her wanted Reba Jean to pay dearly, to feel what she had suffered, but then she realized that Reba Jean did know, for her thoughts had tormented her as well. The mental anguish had been strong for both of them.

Feeling a sick feeling in the pit of her stomach, Reba Jean just sat there in the library, unable to take it all in. Beauty for ashes rang through her mind again; she looked up to see that the golden dust motes were thicker than ever. Then she realized there were no more secrets and no more wooden chests to collect wayward thoughts in any longer. This felt a bit disconcerting but also liberating, but now what? She would have to change the very way she thought about things that upset her. She had been struggling to do this for so very long, but now it had cost her the near demise of the library and its avatar.

The two women sat together for a time, lost in their own thoughts; it was going to take time to recover from this. Reba Jean knew what she was capable of, and it scared her. Lady Jane tried not to be afraid of Reba Jean and her penchant for thoughts that could destroy them both. The light from the oil lamp seemed to chase all the gloom away, and the library warmed under a soft aura of restoration.

Reba Jean noticed the changes, yet she still felt like she was going to be sick; she was sick of herself. Whether the army of the underworld had had a hand in this or not, it was still up to her to be in control of what happened in the library. Look what she had caused to happen! She moaned, still in anguish, and started sobbing again.

Lady Jane wasn't sure what to do. Reba Jean still seemed in torment even though the Overseer had restored her and the library back into working order and even better. Lady Jane looked around trying to figure out if she needed to say or do anything. She spied two beautiful figures coming down the staircase together, and they approached Reba Jean as she sat lost in her anguish over her sin.

Together they surrounded her in their ethereal arms and held her; a third one joined them and began singing over her a celestial song. It was Goodness and Mercy who held Reba Jean, and later she learned it was Grace who sang over her until she was able to be strong again in the Word of the Lord and in the power of His might.

Lady Jane gaped in awe as these beautiful, heavenly helpers ministered to Reba Jean. She couldn't wait to tell Lady Constance about this! Oh, the time they would have discussing this together. She got goosebumps just thinking about how she would jump for joy at the story of these heavenly helpers. The glow of the oil lamp seemed to burn even brighter; the golden dust motes seemed to join in the singing from Grace. It was just amazing... Amazing Grace began to play in her mind. Such a wretch she might look like, but oh, what a wonder she had been transformed into.

Reba Jean felt peace once again reign in her mind and body as the soothing tones of the celestial minstrel faded away back up the staircase. She sat up and looked at the three golden figures surrounding her. They did not speak, yet she could hear their names given to her within her spirit. Goodness and Mercy would follow her all the days of her life, and Grace would be there when she needed him.

She knelt her face to the floor and worshipped her Heavenly Father with a thankful heart.

Lady Jane was in awe; she had heavenly messengers in the library full-time now. Lord Rabboni had sent reinforcements to protect her and to keep the library transforming into His likeness. She joined Reba Jean in worship and praise to King Abba and Lord Rabboni. The very air of the library was full of a sweet scent of worship that is only present when one is transported into the Court of Praise.

Lady Jane remembered Lady Constance asking if there was a court jester in the library. This had disturbed her a bit at the time, but she secretly thought Reba Jean was probably the so-called court jester. She sure did think very foolishly and irreverently. Lady Jane brought her mind back to the present; here she had been praising the King, and her mind slides off into foolishness! Maybe both of them were the court jesters after all.

Reba Jean held her hand out to Lady Jane, who, after a long pause, slowly accepted it. Lady Jane felt like she would not truly be able to trust Reba Jean for a long time, if ever. Reba Jean seemed to understand and acknowledge her unspoken thoughts and bowed her head down in sorrow. It was time for her to go back down to the living room and try to restore some semblance of normalcy in her life.

Her prayers afterward often felt so desperate and pleading; she prayed for her mind, and she prayed for this new puppy that had seemed to be the catalyst for her mental and emotional breakdown. She knew how dangerous it was not to get enough sleep, so she begged God to help her sleep. He graciously answered; she was in awe of how the puppy improved every time she prayed about it disrupting her need to get things accomplished.

The television had to be rebooted to get the internet channels it had somehow lost, and now it had the internet channels and not the regular local channels. Reba Jean tried a few different things and then just took it as a sign that she needed to stop watching television anyway. With thoughts of what had happened in the library still fresh in her mind, she turned on the selection of orchestrated hymns that she loved to play over the sound system. Just minutes later Amazing Grace came on and she about cried. The Lord always made His Presence known; she just had to be attentive to Him. Then, still thinking about the tragic mental results of the weekend, a Scripture verse came to mind. She started looking for the reference so that she could read it again. As she searched through the Epistles, she came across Ephesians 4:23, "And be renewed in the spirit of your mind." This chapter in Ephesians 4 was so clear on how she should live and think according to the perfecting of the saints. She flipped a page and her eyes caught on Ephesians 2:4, "But God, who is rich in mercy, for His great love wherewith He loved us," again seemed to reassure her that He was talking to her both in mind and spirit. Now, where was that Scripture she was looking for? A verse leaped off the pages at her from Colossians 1:21, "And you, that were sometime alienated and enemies in your mind by wicked works, yet now hath He reconciled."

She paused and felt butterflies in her stomach as she realized how totally applicable this verse was! She still hadn't found the reference to the original verse yet; she could do an internet search for it but found that just by skimming through her precious Bible, she was finding parallel nuggets of truth that she would have missed by just doing an online search for it. Another verse reminded her of a previous thought about the word "confidant." Philippians 1:6 "Being confident of this very thing, that He which hath begun a good work in your will perform it until the day of Jesus Christ." Jesus hadn't given up working on her, and she needed to stop giving up on working for Him!

2 Corinthians 12:9, "And He said unto me, My grace is sufficient for thee: for my strength is made perfect in weakness..." Verse after verse seared themselves into her soul as she read the truth of God's Word as it directly applied to her

182

situation. Why did it seem that she always read His Word AFTER the trouble and not through the trouble?

She found it! The verse that had come to her mind as she had left the library earlier. It was 1 Corinthians 10:13, "There hath no temptation taken you but such as is common to man: but God is faithful, who will not suffer you to be tempted above that ye are able; but will with the temptation also make a way to escape, that ye may be able to bear it." She needed to learn the escape routes that He offered instead of falling headlong into the abyss!

Reba Jean folded her hands and meditated on all the verses that she had just read and skimmed through in her search of the Scriptures. All of them were very familiar, most of them had been memorized, yet when the time came to swing her Sword of Truth, she had succumbed in defeat and despair. With the secrets gone, the past locked up, and the recent enemies of the mind banished, why was the Women's Conference such a huge issue still? She had prayed yet again today that it would be a real time of spiritual renewal for all who were connected to it.

It was most likely because she was yearning for true spiritual help and insight more than fellowship and chit-chat. It was fear that it would be a disappointment and feel like a waste of time, money, and stress. She finally put her finger on what was truly the root of her unease. It needed to be more than book material, but she wanted good material to include in this book she was writing. Now that she understood the nagging issue, she could now pray toward that end. The stress over the puppy would also be consistently prayed over.

It was time to attack everything that was an issue with the tried-and-true remedy of the Word and prayer. She bowed her heart in prayer as she committed these situations to the Lord. She so wanted His will, not her selfish desires.

She asked for faith over fear and strength for her weaknesses. She felt empty, and it made her stomach even feel hungry… the spiritual and mental always affected the physical and emotional.

Inhaling a cleansing sigh of relief, she thanked God for the truth He had shown her, and she submitted herself to the Lord. Even if the Women's Conference was a disappointment, it would be a test to see if she had learned her lesson this week. Stretching and pulling on a cloak of confidence, she decided to live victoriously through the Lord Jesus Christ.

Lady Jane could tell things were much different in the library this time; there was such a warm comforting glow emanating from the oil lamp on the rugged table. The space was even roomier without all those crates and chests scattered around. Spotting the barrel of oil, she was reminded of the golden dust motes, and her gaze swung upward. The entire ceiling was aglow with what looked like a galaxy of golden twinkles as the motes seemed to dance merrily around. She stood up gingerly and walked around the various floors of the library. Sir Theo's library was just a quiet hum, and the wall of hope seemed to be even more translucent than even a day ago.

The fountain of living water was bubbling with audible joy, and the Ancient One beckoned to her like an old Friend. She ran down to the Ancient One and watched its pages flip to various Scriptures. The Truth of the Word burned itself into her synapses like a total reboot of the brain, so to speak. She paused as she meditated on what she had seen and read and absorbed. A hush fell over the library, and she felt a familiar sprig of fear only to feel it vanish away as she glanced towards Goodness and Mercy sitting near her. She felt the strength of Grace envelop her, and she knew that things were much different than they had ever been.

For a moment, she remembered Mr. Insidious and Insecurity, and a startling wordplay came to her mind. If she changed the first three letters of each of their names around... They spelled SIN!! She nearly fell over when she realized how easily she had been deceived. She would need to help Reba Jean keep her guard up from now on. It was just as important for her to protect the library that she lived in as much as it was for Reba Jean to keep them safe.

Chapter 17

The forces of the Evil Lord of the Dark Realm gathered for a battle briefing in the Field of Despair. They had seen victory, and most of it, they couldn't honestly take credit for, but they still claimed it as a victory. They had sown seeds, and the fruit was manifested for all to see. Then something seemed to have thrown their whole scheme into a maelstrom. Again, they saw the Celestial forces recapture stolen ground and solidify their bulwarks for the King of the Heavenly Hosts.

Meeting together, they sniffed the air; it was such a sickening, sweet savor instead of the stench of defeat. That Reba Jean was praying AGAIN!! It stunk every time she started her earnest petitions to the King. Their stomachs churned as the Field of Despair turned into Fields of Grace; they screeched as Grace and Mercy and Goodness strode onto the battlefield.

Mr. Insidious sounded the call of retreat, and they slunk off, looking for another in-between space to recalculate their objectives. Shortly, a scout came running back to say that Reba Jean was in the yard with that cursed puppy. Temptation was dispatched with a small troop to attack. With fiery darts, they flung thoughts and suggestions at her. She met each one with a determined thrust of resistance. Nasty thoughts were fired at her, and Reba Jean told them to go away; they were not welcome, nor were they going to be obeyed.

Reba Jean fought against the onslaught, and as she achieved victory through the Lord Jesus Christ, she felt almost as if a cloud of depression had finally left her. She wiped her eyes with shaking hands and pondered on how to keep those fiery darts away. Those unwelcome thoughts were abhorrent, she was tired of fighting them away, but fight them she must.

She walked back inside with the puppy, thinking long and hard about things.

Lady Jane could see the misty tendrils writing in books, she saw the onslaught of the fiery darts, but then they seemed to vanish before doing any damage. Books opened and closed, and normally this would have worried her. Not now, though; she had celestial protection of the next level right there with her. Oh, it wasn't that the Ancient One hadn't been enough; she just loved seeing Grace, Mercy, and Goodness right there with her as visual representations of King Abba's love towards her.

The puppy demanded more of Reba Jean's attention, and the battle seemed to be at an impasse for the moment. Mr. Insidious reminded himself that he played the long game, and there was still time to score more ground for the Evil Lord the rest of the week and most definitely during the Women's Conference this weekend. He did a mental tally of all the recruits he had sent forth and the in-roads that they had managed to make in the demise of Reba Jean. Satisfied that everything was still going as planned, he closed his notes and contemplated his next move. It was all about timing, and it seemed like the little things had a bigger effect than any major trouble.

Reba Jean awoke still sleepy but not frazzled, which was a good thing. She started praying for her husband, and as she had her devotions in 1 Chronicles, it led her back to Genesis 39, and she meditated on how the world had gone astray from its Creator so very long ago. She was then reminded of the pastor she was watching last night who was expounding on the imminent return of the Lord.

Was the purpose of writing this book just to help the author? Lady Constance had told Lady Jane that even if just one person read the book and was helped, how powerful that would be for the Kingdom. We may not know the time of Christ's return to rapture His church, but it was sure to be very

188

soon. Her husband wanted her to stock up in preparation for the possible famine ahead. She felt almost like Joseph, preparing for famine.

As she scrolled disinterestedly through social media, a post caught her attention. It stated to the effect that she could have peace in her heart even if there was chaos running rampant in her mind. This really bothered Reba Jean because it seemed to imply that her mind did not need or was not capable of having peace. This went against everything that she had been fighting for all these years. A transformed mind, a Christlike mind should be a peaceful mind, not full of chaos. God is not the author of confusion or chaos, so why would it be okay to tell people that your heart can have peace but don't expect your mind to have it as well? Now, maybe the intentions of this quote were good on a shallow level, but Reba Jean chose to believe that it was important to let God control your mind, then you can have peace throughout.

Lost in thought, the hymns playing in the background, the pets sleeping, it was a beautiful morning for reflection and introspection. Jesus was most definitely coming soon; would He find her strong in the Lord and in the power of His might? Or would He find her defeated by sin and settling for shallow mediocrity that the so-called religious world was pumping into apathetic sheep?

It was then that she was conscious that the hymn that was playing was "How Great Thou Art," and she closed her eyes in worship along with the hymn. It was good to have a mind at peace, at least for the moment.

Lady Jane heard the sacred music playing over the sound system, the sun streaming through the windows. It was peaceful and sweet in the library this morning; even the dream room was silent and forgotten. She wandered over to the fountain of living water to sprinkle a few drops on her face to freshen up. It was then that she noticed her reflection in the crystal-clear water. She was scarred and marred by the sinful thoughts that had attacked her. There were wrinkles from the anxiety and depression that had weighed so heavily and frequently upon her.

She started to feel resentment and anger well up inside of her; then, as the living water dropped from her fingers onto her face, she remembered how the Overseer had healed her wounds with the Balm of Gilead. The scars were to remind both her and Reba Jean of the consequences of not controlling their thoughts. Resentment, anger, and bitterness would only make her look worse, not better if she let them fester inside of her. The clean freshness of the water soothed her furrowed brow, and she too closed her eyes to listen to the sacred music.

The time had come: the pet sitter was scheduled to arrive later that night, packing the suitcase had begun, some time would be spent working this afternoon, then the mad rush to get ready to leave for the weekend. The long-awaited Women's Conference was about to commence! A backup plan had even been orchestrated should any need arise while she was gone and her husband was at work. All was going well; she was committed to going to see what the Lord would have her learn this weekend. She was determined to practice what she had learned this last month.

Then the bottom fell out! What on earth? Reba Jean was sick with a virus the day before the conference was to begin. A flurry of messages between her and her boss assured her that it was most likely a twenty-four-hour virus, and she should hopefully be fine to go with the group the next day.

Except, she wasn't! She was still sick and completely baffled. The pet sitter was canceled, the extra pair of hands was notified, the suitcase was slowly unpacked, and the days were spent in total befuddlement.

Mr. Insidious and his army were dumbstruck as they learned that Reba Jean was sick, and the whole campaign to bring her down spiritually and maybe even ruin her testimony at the Women's Conference was halted. A flurry of meetings ensued, plans suggested and discarded. Then Guilt put his hand up and volunteered for damage control. Guilt was swiftly dispatched to the upper realm to wreak whatever havoc he could with Reba Jean while she was physically weak.

Reba Jean fought Guilt for three days; he told her often that she never really wanted to go to this meeting. She had looked for all sorts of excuses not to go, and this sickness was all in her head. In fact, it was just a product of her stressing out about going away for the weekend. It was all her fault that she was sick, and when they left without her, she would feel better. Except, she didn't feel better; it was reassuring to find she was still sick and that it wasn't all in her mind or nerves.

She found some natural remedies to try, and slowly Reba Jean felt like she was getting better, at least it was not getting worse. Her mind quieted down, and she had long moments of calm and peace. None of this made sense; she had resolved to go to the Women's Conference. This whole month had been focused on it; it was expected and assumed that all women who were spiritually minded would go to any meeting that would help them to grow, right? She did not believe in coincidences, but the purpose of her staying home was unknown.

Guilt slid in a condemnation that God had kept her home so that she would not be a spiritual deterrent to the other women. Her attitude would be a hindrance; she would be a distraction, and so God kept her home to keep the other women safe. Was this true? She had not even had her devotions yesterday, so she was feeling bereft of any sort of answers.

She was dreading next week; she did not even want to go to church or work. She could feel the guilt and condemnation mounting. She tried to think of reasons why she was allowed to get sick. Maybe she was needed more at home to help her husband while he worked overtime; maybe Guilt was right, and she would have been a hindrance, not a help.

The only good that had come out of this so far was that she had barely been on social media. She had, however, watched way too much television as she curled up on the chaise lounge in misery. Then, to top it off, she had been bitten on the back of her hip by something, and it had caused a huge welt. So, Reba Jean was sick and now had a boil, reminding her of Job and Hezekiah from the Bible.

Wondering how Lady Jane was in the middle of all this befuddlement, Reba Jean slowly climbed the staircase, trying not to be sick as she opened the door to the library. Once inside, it was very calm and quiet, which was odd in and of itself. She slowly looked around, and all seemed as she had left it days ago. Hearing a strange noise, though, she inched along a corridor that seemed out of place to investigate. The dream room had moved location and was now down this long corridor. Standing in the doorway in morbid fascination was Lady Jane. Her eyes were glued to the myriad of macabre scenes playing out in the room. She jumped when Reba Jean touched her on the arm. They looked at the scenes together for a minute and then stared at each other in wide-eyed horror. Reba Jean's dreams were always so bizarre and often seemed to have a life of their own. For a few days, they had been easily analyzed and archived. Last night's dream was harder to figure out. It was of people having affairs, committing suicide, leaving children without parents, engagements, illegitimate pregnancies, and all happening to people she knew. What in the world was going on with her mind? How did it conjure up so much weirdness?

The two women sat down in the corridor with their backs to the scenes playing in a loop in the dream room. They shook their heads at each other simultaneously. Shrugging their shoulders, they sat quietly, each lost in their own thoughts. Reba Jean leaned her head against the porous wall behind her and felt it throbbing. The sound of the dishwasher and the air conditioner could be heard from outside the library. The sun was shining brightly through the windows overhead. There was a stillness in spite of the throbbing; it was almost peaceful, yet there was a touch of expectation hovering around the edges.

She looked up, half expecting to see an odd shoe floating around waiting to drop. No, it wasn't quite like that, but there did seem to be an almost foreboding calm of sorts signaling possibly an impending storm. Guilt did not seem to have followed her into the library. Was her mind a safe haven for once? Reba Jean giggled at the thought, startling Lady Jane from her reverie.

Lady Jane was enjoying the calm outside of the dream room. She knew that Reba Jean did not feel well. She was relieved that they were just home for a quiet weekend. She had not relished the influx of thoughts and emotions that would have transpired from Reba Jean having to deal with people all weekend. Reba Jean might be fighting to be "normal," but Lady Jane knew that as much as the anxiety and stress were seemingly under control, they always came back to overwhelm them both.

They missed the Presence of the Overseer and longed for His assurance and comfort that King Abba and Lord Rabboni knew what was going to happen. Were they in trouble for their thoughts? Was this sickness a chastisement? Reba Jean felt her stomach roil; was she making herself sick? All these unanswered questions were like secrets being kept from her. Now what?

A soft answer seemed to encourage her to rest and restore her relationship with the King as she had not been in His Word much, and time would reveal what He wanted her to know. She sat in the quiet thinking about this; she knew it was time to finish the book and do a thorough edit before turning it over to the publisher.

Again, she had to trust God that He wanted this book written, so deleting it was not an option. Giving it to a publisher that she was acquainted with was, however, not comforting. All her life, she had been told she was weird; she had learned to accept that, no matter the effort and attempts to fit into some sort of cookie-cutter Christian mold.

Guilt had built on what Doubtful, Anxiety, and Insecurity had started. He laid it on really thick for two days. Then, Reba Jean had gone to the library, and he found he could not seem to get in. There was a special lock on the door. He sent down for reinforcements. An army of creepy, nasty creatures rose from the depths of the nether world to bombard the library.

Reba Jean knew that when she was physically weak that the enemy was able to have a stronger impact on her. She wondered about the dreams and realized that maybe they were just a small by-product of all the horrid thoughts that had come to her mind in the last week. She was appalled at the abhorrent thoughts that had attacked her. However, she kept hearing the verse that said, "Resist the devil, and he will flee from you," running through her mind. So, every time something abominable would suggest itself to her, she would mentally shout "NO! Go Away," and it would! She just had to keep resisting, even though the shock of some of the thoughts made her think she would go to hell after all. She definitely deserved it.

Mr. Insidious led the onslaught from his band; he needed to cripple Reba Jean, reclaim Lady Jane and the library, and render both women useless for his enemy, the King of the Heavenly Realm. He had an endless army and a vast arsenal of fiery darts. He saw her resist but was not deterred. He would just retreat and then attack from another side. Victory was close; he could taste her defeat like sweet, decadent human failure always tasted.

He did not know why she did not get to go to the Women's Conference either, but he would just use that to his advantage, as well. She was home and isolated; he would remind her that she was anti-social and that even her family and friends didn't really care, or they would check on her. They only used her for their selfish needs; she was alone and even God was chastising her.

Looking for other ways into the library since the door was locked, he sent his army to attack the porous walls and see if access could be acquired through the channels attached to the sound system. The sacred music wasn't playing; he could send his dark evil spirits upon her while she wasn't protected. It was just like King Saul of ancient times, he mused.

Reba Jean felt the throbbing of the walls increase, the roar of the air conditioner seemed louder, and a restlessness overcame her. Sitting here with Lady Jane had seemed safe, but now it felt like her head was going to split wide open. She tried to pray, but there just seemed to be a wall of sorts. Waiting was what she had been told to do just a few minutes before, so waiting is what she needed to do. She told herself to just stop thinking about everything.

Reaching over to Lady Jane, she squeezed her hand and rose to leave the library. Lady Jane was obviously in better condition than she herself was. It was just such an odd stillness around her; the waiting was unsettling. This prayer thing was disturbing; it was time to find out how to tear that wall down. She would need help with all the attacks of the wicked one.

Reba Jean exited the library and went directly to her rarely used prayer closet. Oh, she prayed, and often, but she had not been in her prayer closet itself for days. She did not feel good, and her head was aching, but there was something amiss in her spiritual side that needed to be corrected.

Chapter 18

Weeks—long torturous weeks—had passed; every time she had tried to work on the book it was interrupted. Her self-imposed deadline had passed, but she was here finally finishing the last chapter and editing. Fear of going to the library and seeing if her reality had destroyed it had kept her from checking on it and Lady Jane. Each day had been full of the same old demonic forces, and too many times, she had fallen in defeat. She only hoped her mind had not been permanently damaged from the horrific onslaught. It was sad to say the same issues were still the same issues; every victory was followed by defeat. The cycle was never ending and seemingly futile. Depression and resentment had dogged her daily life; she still struggled to get enough sleep.

Goodness and Mercy and Grace only seemed to be visible in the library; she hoped they had protected Lady Jane from the horrific demonic attacks that had happened in the last few weeks. Wounded, scarred, and bewildered about why she was always fighting the same battles over again, left her questioning everything.

With great reluctance, she climbed to the library, her shoulders slumped and her expression downcast. Maybe the library was fine, and she could bask in the peace that might still be there. Oh, how she longed for the vicious cycle to end. Opening the door to the version of reality was going to be heartbreaking if all she found was a representation of her reprehensible thoughts.

Slipping inside, she immediately climbed the spiral staircase to look back out the windows. Spying hummingbirds flitting about and sunshine pouring through the crystal blue windows, she inhaled deeply, steeling herself before turning about to survey the library from above. Three golden figures were visible as they worked to repair a very damaged battlefield. Remnants of resisted fiery darts were being removed, missiles were being disarmed, and the Golden Sword of the Ancient One was sweeping away incoming enemy fire.

Lady Jane had a mop that she had dipped into the fountain of living water and was busy washing away soot and ash and gore. It had been hard work the last few weeks; Reba Jean had been fighting so many battles and feeling defeated. The library had held its own, but not without significant damage. Not even hearing or sensing that Reba Jean was on the premises, the cleanup had to be done, and Lady Jane cared enough to be undeterred from completing it.

Reba Jean heard the Ancient One flip its pages, beckoning her to its golden script. The pages had opened to a well-known passage in 1 Chronicles 4:10. "And Jabez called on the God of Israel, saying, Oh that thou wouldest bless me indeed, and enlarge my coast, and that thine hand might be with me, and that thou wouldest keep me from evil, that it may not grieve me! And God granted him that which he requested."

The prayer of Jabez was used by so many to claim riches in Jesus' name or in missions to expand their outreach, but the phrase that leaped out at her was the last part of his prayer. She had NEVER heard this part, "that thou wouldest keep me from evil, that it may not grieve me!" To her, that was the most powerful part of the prayer! That was exactly what she needed, to be kept from evil so that it would not grieve her. Oh, how grieved she had been by the evil attacks on her mind and body.

The minions of the dark realm had reduced her to a resentment-filled failure with mommy issues. Sitting on the floor under the Ancient One, she pulled out the book she was finishing and penned in the verse.

Her mind wandered over the past few weeks, so many of her friends and family were all dealing with various issues in their libraries. She needed to be in much prayer for them as they needed the strength and wisdom to handle the stresses of life.

Noticing a book laying near her, she looked as it opened to a page that had a lot of erasures and re-written words on it. A drawing of sunshine kept appearing and disappearing on the page. It was with a realization that even though the thought of not including certain characters in her book was all well and good in theory, the reality of it was that once thought, it was going to be in a book in the library.

Sitting still, she looked around the library as the cleanup was nearing completion yet again. The battlefield of her own mind was a reminder that the war was still raging. Bowing her head, she prayed the version of the prayer of Jabez as it applied to her. "Oh, Lord, God of Heaven, please keep me from evil, that it may not grieve me!"

Dear Reader,

I hope it has been as much of a joy for you to read this book as it was for us to publish it. I also hope you have not just enjoyed the story but also considered the message. If you are saved, the battle for your soul is over, but the battle for your mind has only just begun! So, in the power of the Holy Spirit, guard your mind, and in so doing, guard your heart, your life, and your home.

And if you do not yet know Christ as your Savior, why wait another day? Romans 10:13 says, "For whosoever shall call upon the name of the Lord shall be saved." So, why don't you call on Him?

Your prayer can be as simple as, "Lord Jesus, I am so sorry for my sin, and I am asking you to please forgive me. I know you rose from the dead, and I freely give you my life to control."

A person who truly prays that to God, from the heart, will be born again and have the most wonderful Overseer, the Holy Ghost, move into them to help them along the way.

Pastor Bo Wagner
Word of His Mouth Publishers

Coming Soon

Reba Jean felt her anxiety claw at her as she began racing through the library searching for Lady Jane. She did not dare call out, and she really had no reason for the unexplained fear that gripped her vocal cords. Racing up the stairs to the various levels and frantically searching corridors and dimly lit corners, she found the crevice that had sucked Lady Jane into the Sea of Despair. Only a bricked wall blocked the portal to the underworld. The celestial companions were not visible, the artifacts were in their places; it didn't appear that the library was under siege. Where was Lady Jane?!

The usual places were empty; even Sir Theo's library was quiet except for the steady hum of his bees working away with their data storage. She did not seek answers from the Ancient One or use the oil Lamp to help her search. The Golden Swords lay inert, the fountain only bubbled sporadically, and Lady Jane was just GONE! The puppy nosed around interested in its own treasure hunt and did not seem to realize that anything was amiss. Where was Lady Jane? If Lady Jane was gone, did that mean she had lost her mind?

Captain Insidious had assembled his drowned rats and sent them through the sulphuric lava pits, where the black ooze of the underworld would refortify them with rebellion, resentment, anger, temptation, etc. The tar pits seared the wounds the living water had left on his rat brigade, now he could dispatch them to other targets. Sitting with his military counsel, he pulled out the manual on how to rob a Christian. The manual stated that their testimony was the ultimate goal to tarnish and steal from them. "Ok, you scallywags, let's be the pirates that she thinks we are; it's time to go pillage and destroy!"

Armed with knowledge from centuries of research, Captain Insidious knew that he had to attack and steal Reba Jean's sanity, security, surety, story, and steadfastness. He read all the "s" words and his hiss increased intensely. Oh, how he loved "S" words; they slithered off his tongue so deliciously. *How ssssatisssfying, this quest would be*, thought Captain Insidious.

Made in the USA
Middletown, DE
15 October 2023

40797808R00125